Ernest Christopher Dowson

Dilemmas

stories and studies in sentiment

Ernest Christopher Dowson

Dilemmas
stories and studies in sentiment

ISBN/EAN: 9783337396626

Printed in Europe, USA, Canada, Australia, Japan

Cover: Foto ©Andreas Hilbeck / pixelio.de

More available books at **www.hansebooks.com**

DILEMMAS

STORIES AND STUDIES IN SENTIMENT

*The Diary of a Successful Man—A Case of
Conscience—An Orchestral Violin—
Souvenirs of an Egoist—The
Statute of Limitations*

BY

ERNEST DOWSON

LONDON
ELKIN MATHEWS
NEW YORK
FREDERICK A. STOKES COMPANY
MDCCCXCV

TO

MISSIE

(A. F.)

Certain of these pieces have appeared in *Macmillan's Magazine*, *Temple Bar*, and the *Hobby Horse*, to the courtesy of whose editors I am indebted for permission to republish them in this form.

CONTENTS

THE DIARY OF A SUCCESSFUL
MAN

1st October, 188—

Hotel du Lys, Bruges.

AFTER all, few places appeal to my imagination more potently than this autumnal old city— the most mediaeval town in Europe. I am glad that I have come back here at last. It is melancholy indeed, but then at my age one's pleasures are chiefly melancholy. One is essentially of the autumn, and it is always autumn at Bruges. I thought I had been given back my youth when I awoke this morning and heard the Carillon, chiming out, as it has done, no doubt, intermittently, since I heard it last—twenty years ago. Yes, for a moment, I thought I was young again —only for a moment. When I went out into the streets and resumed acquaintance with all my old haunts, the illusion had gone. I strolled into Saint Sauveur's, wandered a while through its dim, dusky aisles, and then sat down near the

high altar, where the air was heaviest with stale
incense, and indulged in retrospect.   I was
there for more than an hour. I doubt whether
it was quite wise. At my time of life one had
best keep out of cathedrals ; they are vault-like
places, pregnant with rheumatism—at best they
are full of ghosts. And a good many *revenants*
visited me during that hour of meditation.
Afterwards I paid a visit to the Memlings in the
Hôpital. Nothing has altered very much ; even
the women, with their placid, ugly Flemish faces,
sitting eternally in their doorways with the
eternal lace-pillow, might be the same women.
In the afternoon I went to the Béguinage, and
sat there long in the shadow of a tree, which
must have grown up since my time, I think. I
sat there too long, I fear, until the dusk and the
chill drove me home to dinner. On the whole
perhaps it was a mistake to come back. The
sameness of this terribly constant old city seems
to intensify the change that has come to oneself.
Perhaps if I had come back with Lorimer I
should have noticed it less. For, after all, the
years have been kind to me, on the whole; they
have given me most things which I set my heart
upon, and if they had not broken a most perfect
friendship, I would forgive them the rest. I

sometimes feel, however, that one sacrifices too much to one's success. To slave twenty years at the Indian bar has its drawbacks, even when it does leave one at fifty, prosperous *à mourir d'ennui*. Yes, I must admit that I am prosperous, disgustingly prosperous, and—my wife is dead, and Lorimer—Lorimer has altogether passed out of my life. Ah, it is a mistake to keep a journal—a mistake.

3rd October.

I vowed yesterday that I would pack my portmanteau and move on to Brussels, but to-day finds me still at Bruges. The charm of the old Flemish city grows on me. To-day I carried my peregrinations further a-field. I wandered about the Quais and stood on the old bridge where one obtains such a perfect glimpse, through a trellis of chestnuts, of the red roof and spires of Notre Dame. But the particular locality matters nothing ; every nook and corner of Bruges teems with reminiscences. And how fresh they are ! At Bombay I had not time to remember or to regret ; but to-day the whole dead and forgotten story rises up like a ghost to haunt me. At times, moreover, I have a curious, fan-tastic feeling, that some day or other, in some mildewing church, I shall come face to face with Lorimer. He was older than I, he must be greatly altered, but I should know him. It is strange how intensely I desire to meet him. I suppose it is chiefly curiosity. I should like to feel sure of him, to explain his silence. He cannot be dead. I am told that he had pictures in this last Academy—and yet, never to have written—never once, through all these years. I suppose there are few friendships which can stand the test of correspondence. Still it is inexplicable, it is not like Lorimer. He could not have harboured a grudge against me—for what? A boyish infatuation for a woman who adored him, and whom he adored. The idea is preposterous, they must have laughed over my folly often, of winter evenings by their fireside. For they married, they must have married, they were made for each other and they knew it. Was their marriage happy I wonder? Was it as successful as mine, though perhaps a little less commonplace? It is strange, though, that I never heard of it, that he never wrote to me once, not through all those years.

4th October.

Inexplicable ! Inexplicable ! *Did* they marry

after all? Could there have been some gigantic
misunderstanding? I paid a pilgrimage this
morning which hitherto I had deferred, I know
not precisely why. I went to the old house in
the Rue d'Alva—where she lived, our Comtesse.
And the sight of its grim, historic frontal made
twenty years seem as yesterday. I meant to
content myself with a mere glimpse at the barred
windows, but the impulse seized me to ring the
bell which I used to ring so often. It was a
foolish, fantastic impulse, but I obeyed it. I
found it was occupied by an Englishman, a Mr
Venables—there seem to be more English here
than in my time—and I sent in my card and
asked if I might see the famous dining-room.
There was no objection raised, my host was
most courteous, my name, he said, was familiar
to him ; he is evidently proud of his dilapidated
old palace, and has had the grace to save it from
the attentions of the upholsterer. No! twenty
years have produced very little change in the room
where we had so many pleasant sittings. The
ancient stamped leather on the walls is perhaps
a trifle more ragged, the old oak panels not
blacker—that were impossible—but a trifle more
worm-eaten ; it is the same room. I must have
seemed a sad boor to my polite cicerone as I

stood, hat in hand, and silently took in all the old familiar details. The same smell of mildewed antiquity, I could almost believe the same furniture. And indeed my host tells me that he took over the house as it was, and that some of the chairs and tables are scarcely more youthful than the walls. Yes, there by the huge fireplace was the same quaintly carved chair where she always sat. Ah, those delicious evenings when one was five-and-twenty. For the moment I should not have been surprised if she had suddenly taken shape before my eyes, in the old seat, the slim, girlish woman in her white dress, her hands folded in her lap, her quiet eyes gazing dreamily into the red fire, a subtile air of distinction in her whole posture. . . . . She would be old now, I suppose. Would she? Ah no, she was not one of the women who grow old. . . . . I caught up the thread of my host's discourse just as he was pointing it with a sharp rap upon one of the most time-stained panels.

'Behind there,' he remarked, with pardonable pride, 'is the secret passage where the Duc d'Alva was assassinated.'

I smiled apologetically.

'Yes,' I said, 'I know it. I should explain perhaps—my excuse for troubling you was not

.

merely hostoric curiosity.   I have more personal
associations with this room.   I spent some charming hours in it a great many years ago—' and for
the moment I had forgotten that I was nearly
fifty.

'Ah,' he said, with interest, 'you know the
late people, the Fontaines.'

'No,' I said, 'I am afraid I have never heard
of them.   I am very ancient.   In my time it be-
longed to the Savaresse family.'

'So I have heard,' he said, 'but that was long
ago.   I have only had it a few years.   Fontaine
my landlord bought it from them.   Did you
know M. le Comte !'

'No,' I answered, 'Madame la Comtesse.   She
was left a widow very shortly after her marriage.
I never knew M. le Comte.'

My host shrugged his shoulders.

'From all accounts,' he said, 'you did not lose
very much.'

'It was an unhappy marriage,' I remarked,
vaguely, 'most unhappy.   Her second marriage
promised greater felicity.'

Mr Venables looked at me curiously.

'I understood,' he begun, but he broke off
abruptly.   'I did not know Madame de Savaresse
married again.'

His tone had suddenly changed, it had grown less cordial, and we parted shortly afterwards with a certain constraint. And as I walked home pensively curious, his interrupted sentence puzzled me. Does he look upon me as an impostor, a vulgar gossip-monger? What has he heard, what does he know of her? Does he know anything? I cannot help believing so. I almost wish I had asked him definitely, but he would have misunderstood my motives. Yet, even so, I wish I had asked him.

6th October.

I am still living constantly in the past, and the fantastic feeling, whenever I enter a church or turn a corner that I shall meet Lorimer again, has grown into a settled conviction. Yes, I shall meet him, and in Bruges. . . . It is strange how an episode which one has thrust away out of sight and forgotten for years will be started back into renewed life by the merest trifle. And for the last week it has all been as vivid as if it happened yesterday. To-night I have been putting questions to myself—so far with no very satisfactory answer. *Was* it a boyish infatuation after all? Has it passed away as utterly as I believed? I can see her face now as I sit by the

fire with the finest precision of detail. I can
hear her voice, that soft, low voice, which was
none the less sweet for its modulation of sadness. I think there are no women like her now-
a-days—none, none! *Did* she marry Lorimer?
and if not—? It seems strange now that we
should have both been so attracted, and yet not
strange when one considers it. At least we were
never jealous of one another. How the details
rush back upon one! I think we must have
fallen in love with her at the same moment—for
we were together when we saw her for the first
time, we were together when we went first to
call on her in the Rue d'Alva—I doubt if we
ever saw her except together. It was soon after
we began to get intimate that she wore white
again. She told us that we had given her back
her youth. She joined our sketching expeditions
with the most supreme contempt for *les conven-
ances;* when she was not fluttering round, passing
from Lorimer's canvas to mine with her sweetly
inconsequent criticism, she sat in the long grass
and read to us—André Chénier and Lamartine.
In the evening we went to see her; she denied
herself to the rest of the world, and we sat for
hours in that ancient room in the delicious twi-
light, while she sang to us—she sang divinely

—little French *chansons*, gay and sad, and snatches of *operette*. How we adored her! I think she knew from the first how it would be and postponed it as long as she could. But at last she saw that it was inevitable. . . . I remember the last evening that we were there —remember—shall I ever forget it? We had stayed beyond our usual hour and when we rose to go we all of us knew that those pleasant irresponsible evenings had come to an end. And both Lorimer and I stood for a moment on the threshold before we said good-night, feeling I suppose that one of us was there for the last time.

And how graceful, how gracious she was as she held out one little white hand to Lorimer and one to me. 'Good-night, dear friends,' she said, 'I like you both so much—so much. Believe me, I am grateful to you both—for having given me back my faith in life, in friendship, believe that, will you not, *mes amis?*' Then for just one delirious moment her eyes met mine and it seemed to me—ah, well, after all it was Lorimer she loved.

7th October.

It seems a Quixotic piece of folly now, our proposal we would neither take advantage of the other, but we both of us *must* speak. We wrote to her at the same time and likely enough, in the same words, we posted our letters by the same post. To-day I had the curiosity to take out her answer to me from my desk, and I read it quite calmly and dispassionately, the poor yellow letter with the faded ink, which wrote 'Finis' to my youth and made a man of me.

'*Pauvre cher Ami,*' she wrote to me, and when I had read that, for the first time in my life and the only time Lorimer's superiority was bitter to me. The rest I deciphered through scalding tears.

'*Pauvre cher Ami,* I am very sorry for you, and yet I think you should have guessed and have spared yourself this pain, and me too a little. No, my friend, that which you ask of me is impossible. You are my dear friend, but it is your brother whom I love—your brother, for are you not as brothers, and I can not break your beautiful friendship. No, that must not be. See, I ask one favour of you—I have written also to him, only one little word " Viens,"—but will you not go to him and tell him for me? Ah, my brother, my heart bleeds for you. I too have suffered in my time. You will go away now,

yes, that is best, but you will return when this
fancy of yours has passed.   Ah forgive me—that
I am happy—forgive us, forgive me.   Let us
still be friends.   Adieu !   Au revoir.

' Thy Sister,

'DELPHINE.'

I suppose it was about an hour later that I
took out my letter to Lorimer.   I told him as I
told myself, that it was the fortune of war, that
she had chosen the better man, but I could not
bear to stay and see their happiness.   I was in
London before the evening.   I wanted work,
hard, grinding work, I was tired of being a brief-
less barrister, and as it happened, an Indian
opening offered itself at the very moment when
I had decided that Europe had become impossible
to me.   I accepted it, and so those two happy
ones passed out of my life.

Twenty years ago ! and in spite of his promise
he has never written from that day till this, not
so much as a line to tell me of his marriage.
I made a vow then that I would get over my
folly, and it seemed to me that my vow was
kept.   And yet here to-day, in Bruges, I am
asking myself whether after all it has been such

a great success, whether sooner or later one does not have to pay for having been hard and strong, for refusing to suffer. . . . I must leave this place, it is too full of Madame de Savaresse. . . . Is it curiosity which is torturing me ? I *must* find Lorimer. If he married her, why has he been so persistently silent ? If he did not marry her, what in Heaven's name does it mean ? These are vexing questions.

10*th October.*

In the Church of the Dames Rouges, I met to-day my old friend Sebastian Lorimer. Strange ! Strange ! He was greatly altered, I wonder almost that I recognised him. I had strolled into the church for benediction, for the first time since I have been back here, and when the service was over and I swung back the heavy door, with the exquisite music of the 'O Salutaris,' sung by those buried women behind the screen still echoing in my ear, I paused a moment to let a man pass by me. It was Lorimer, he looked wild and worn ; it was no more than the ghost of my old friend. I was shocked and startled by his manner. We shook hands quite impassively as if we had parted yesterday. He talked in a rambling way as we walked towards my hotel, of the singing of the nuns, of the numerous religious processions, of the blessed doctrine of the intercession of saints. The old melodious voice was unchanged, but it was pitched in the singularly low key which I have noticed some foreign priests acquire who live much in churches. I gather that he has become a Catholic. I do not know what intangible instinct, or it may be fear, prevented me from putting to him the vital question which has so perplexed me. It is astonishing how his face has changed, what an extraordinary restlessness his speech and eye have acquired. It never was so of old. My first impression was that he was suffering from some acute form of nervous disorder, but before I left him a more unpleasant suspicion was gradually forced upon me. I cannot help thinking that there is more than a touch of insanity in my old friend. I tried from time to time to bring him down to personal topics, but he eluded them dexterously, and it was only for a moment or so that I could keep him away from the all absorbing subject of the Catholic Church, which seems in some of its more sombre aspects to exercise an extraordinary fascination over him. I asked him if he often visited Bruges.

He looked up at me with a curious expression of surprise.

'I live here,' he said, ' almost always.' I have done so for years. . . .' Presently he added hurriedly, 'You have come back. I thought you would come back, but you have been gone a long time—oh, a long time! It seems years since we met. Do you remember—?' He checked himself; then he added in a low whisper, 'We all come back, we all come back.'

He uttered a quaint, short laugh.

'One can be near—very near, even if one can never be quite close.'

He tells me that he still paints, and that the Academy, to which he sends a picture yearly, has recently elected him an Associate. But his art does not seem to absorb him as it did of old, and he speaks of his success drily and as a matter of very secondary importance. He refused to dine with me, alleging an engagement, but that so hesitatingly and with such vagueness that I could perceive it was the merest pretext. His manner was so strange and remote that I did not venture to press him. I think he is unhappily conscious of his own frequent incoherencies and at moments there are quite painful pauses when he is obviously struggling with dumb piteousness

B

to be lucid, to collect himself and pick up certain lost threads in his memory. He is coming to see me this evening, at his own suggestion, and I am waiting for him now with a strange terror oppressing me. I cannot help thinking that he possesses the key to all that has so puzzled me, and that to-night he will endeavour to speak.

11th October.

Poor Lorimer! I have hardly yet got over the shock which his visit last night caused me, and the amazement with which I heard and read between the lines of his strange confession. His once clear reason is, I fear, hopelessly obscured, and how much of his story is hallucination, I cannot say. His notions of time and place are quite confused, and out of his rambling statement I can only be sure of one fact. It seems that he has done me a great wrong, an irreparable wrong, which he has since bitterly repented.

And in the light of this poor wretch's story, a great misunderstanding is rolled away, and I am left with the conviction that the last twenty years have been after all a huge blunder, an irrevocable and miserable mistake. Through my own rash precipitancy and Lorimer's weak treachery, a trivial mischance that a single word would have rectified, has been prolonged beyond hope of redress. It seems that after all it was not Lorimer whom she chose. Madame de Savaresse writing to us both twenty years ago, made a vital and yet not inexplicable mistake. She confused her envelopes, and the letter which I received was never meant for me, although it was couched in such ambiguous terms that until to-day the possibility of this error never dawned on me. And my letter, the one little word of which she spoke, was sent to Lorimer. Poor wretch ! he did me a vital injury—yes, I can say that now—a vital injury, but on the whole I pity him. To have been suddenly dashed down from the pinnacles of happiness, it must have been a cruel blow. He tells me that when he saw her that afternoon and found out his mistake, he had no thought except to recall me. He actually came to London for that purpose, vowed to her solemnly that he would bring me back; it was only in England, that, to use his own distraught phrase, the Devil entered into possession of him. His half-insane ramblings gave me a very vivid idea of that fortnight during which he lay hid in London, trembling like a guilty thing, fearful at every moment that he might run across me and yet half longing for the

meeting with the irresoluteness of the weak
nature, which can conceive and to a certain
extent execute a *lâcheté*, yet which would
always gladly yield to circumstance and let
chance or fate decide the issue. And to the
very last Lorimer was wavering—had almost
sought me out, and thrown himself on my
mercy, when the news came that I had sailed.

Destiny who has no weak scruples, had stepped
in and sealed Delphine's mistake for all time,
after her grim fashion. When he went back to
Bruges, and saw Madame de Savaresse, I think
she must have partly guessed his baseness.
Lorimer was not strong enough to be a successful
hypocrite, and that meeting, I gather, was also
their final parting. She must have said things
to him in her beautiful quiet voice which he has
never forgotten. He went away and each day he
was going to write to me, and each day he deferred it, and then he took up the *Times* one
morning and read the announcement of my
marriage. After that it seemed to him that he
could only be silent. . . .

Did *she* know of it too? Did she suffer or did
she understand? Poor woman! poor woman!
I wonder if she consoled herself, as I did, and if so
how she looks back on her success? I wonder

whether she is happy, whether she is dead? I suppose these are questions which will remain unanswered. And yet when Lorimer left me at a late hour last night, it seemed to me that the air was full of unspoken words. Does he know anything of her now! I have a right to ask him these things. And to-morrow I am to meet him, he made the request most strangely—at the same place where we fell in with each other to-day—until to-morrow then!

12th October.

I have just left Sebastian Lorimer at the Church of the Dames Rouges. I hope I was not cruel, but there are some things which one can neither forget nor forgive, and it seemed to me that when I knew the full measure of the ruin he had wrought, my pity for him withered away. 'I hope, Lorimer,' I said, 'that we may never meet again.' And, honestly, I can not forgive him. If she had been happy, if she had let time deal gently with her—ah yes, even if she were dead—it might be easier. But that this living entombment, this hopeless death in life should befall her, she so magnificently fitted for life's finer offices, ah, the pity of it, the pity of it! . . . . But let me set down the whole sad story as it dawned upon me this afternoon in that unearthly church. I was later than the hour appointed ; vespers were over and a server, taper in hand, was gradually transforming the gloom of the high altar into a blaze of light. With a strange sense of completion I took my place next to the chair by which Lorimer, with bowed head, was kneeling, his eyes fixed with a strange intentness on the screen which separated the outer worshippers from the chapel or gallery which was set apart for the nuns. His lips moved from time to time spasmodically, in prayer or ejaculation : then as the jubilant organ burst out, and the officiating priest in his dalmatic of cloth of gold passed from the sacristy and genuflected at the altar, he seemed to be listening in a very passion of attention. But as the incense began to fill the air, and the Litany of Loreto smote on my ear to some sorrowful, undulating Gregorian, I lost thought of the wretched man beside me; I forgot the miserable mistake that he had perpetuated, and I was once more back in the past—with Delphine—kneeling by her side. Strophe by strophe that perfect litany rose and was lost in a cloud of incense, in the mazy arches of the roof.

> 'Janua cœli,
> Stella matutina,
> Salus infirmorum, Ora pro nobis!'

Instrophe and antistrophe: the melancholy, nasal intonation of the priest died away, and the exquisite women's voices in the gallery took it up with exultation, and yet with something like a sob—a sob of limitation.

> 'Refugium peccatorum,
> Consolatrix afflictorum,
> Auxilium Christianorum, Ora pro nobis!'

And so on through all the exquisite changes of the hymn, until the time of the music changed, and the priest intoned the closing line.

> 'Ora pro nobis, Sancta Dei Genetrix!'

and the voices in the gallery answered:

> 'Ut digni efficiamur promissionibus Christi.'

There was one voice which rose above all the others, a voice of marvellous sweetness and power, which from the first moment had caused me a curious thrill. And presently Lorimer bent down and whispered to me: 'So near,' he murmured, 'and yet so far away—so near, and yet never quite close!'

But before he had spoken I had read in his

rigid face, in his eyes fixed with such a passion
of regret on the screen, why we were there—
whose voice it was we had listened to.

I rose and went out of the church quietly
and hastily; I felt that to stay there one moment
longer would be suffocation. . . . Poor woman!
so this is how she sought consolation, in religion!
Well, there are different ways for different
persons—and for me—what is there left for me?
Oh, many things, no doubt, many things. Still,
for once and for the last time, let me set myself
down as a dreary fraud. I never forgot her, not
for one hour or day, not even when it seemed
to me that I had forgotten her most, not even
when I married. No woman ever represented
to me the same idea as Madame de Savaresse.
No woman's voice was ever sweet to me after
hers, the touch of no woman's hand ever made
my heart beat one moment quicker for pleasure
or for pain, since I pressed hers for the last
time on that fateful evening twenty years ago.
Even so—! . . .

When the service was over and the people
had streamed out and dispersed, I went back
for the last time into the quiet church. A
white robed server was extinguishing the last
candle on the altar; only the one red light

perpetually vigilant before the sanctuary, made more visible the deep shadows everywhere.

Lorimer was still kneeling with bowed head in his place. Presently he rose and came towards me. 'She was there—Delphine—you heard her. Ah, Dion, she loves you, she always loves you, you are avenged.'

I gather that for years he has spent hours daily in this church, to be near her, and hear her voice, the magnificent voice rising above all the other voices in the chants of her religion. But he will never see her, for is she not of the Dames Rouges? And I remember now all the stories of the Order, of its strictness, its austerity, its perfect isolation. And chiefly, I remember how they say that only twice after one of these nuns has taken her vows is she seen of anyone except those of her community; once, when she enters the Order, the door of the convent is thrown back and she is seen for a single moment in the scarlet habit of the Order, by the world, by all who care to gaze; and once more, at the last, when clad in the same coarse red garb, they bear her out quietly, in her coffin, into the church.

And of this last meeting, Lorimer, I gather, is always restlessly expectant, his whole life concentrated, as it were, in a very passion of waiting for a moment which will surely come. His theory, I confess, escapes me, nor can I guess how far a certain feverish remorse, an intention of expiation may be set as a guiding spring in his unhinged mind, and account, at least in part, for the fantastic attitude which he must have adopted for many years. If I cannot forgive him, at least I bear him no malice, and for the rest, our paths will hardly cross again. One takes up one's life and expiates its errors, each after one's several fashion—and my way is not Lorimer's. And now that it is all so clear, there is nothing to keep me here any longer, nothing to bring me back again. For it seemed to me to-day, strangely enough, as though a certain candle of hope, of promise, of pleasant possibilities, which had flickered with more or less light for so many years, had suddenly gone out and left me alone in utter darkness, as the knowledge was borne in upon me that henceforth Madame de Savaresse had passed altogether and finally out of my life.

And so to-morrow—Brussels!

A CASE OF CONSCIENCE

I

It was in Brittany, and the apples were already acquiring a ruddier, autumnal tint, amid their greens and yellows, though Autumn was not yet; and the country lay very still and fair in the sunset which had befallen, softly and suddenly as is the fashion there. A man and a girl stood looking down in silence at the village, Ploumariel, from their post of vantage, half way up the hill : at its lichened church spire, dotted with little gables, like dove-cotes; at the slated roof of its market; at its quiet white houses. The man's eyes rested on it complacently, with the enjoyment of the painter, finding it charming : the girl's, a little absently, as one who had seen it very often before. She was pretty and very young, but her gray serious eyes, the poise of her head, with its rebellious brown hair braided

plainly, gave her a little air of dignity, of reserve
which sat piquantly upon her youth. In one
ungloved hand, that was brown from the sun,
but very beautiful, she held an old parasol, the
other played occasionally with a bit of purple
heather. Presently she began to speak, using
English just coloured by a foreign accent, that
made her speech prettier.

'You make me afraid,' she said, turning her
large, troubled eyes on her companion, 'you
make me afraid, of myself chiefly, but a little of
you. You suggest so much to me that is new,
strange, terrible. When you speak, I am troubled;
all my old landmarks appear to vanish; I even
hardly know right from wrong. I love you,
my God, how I love you! but I want to go
away from you and pray in the little quiet
church, where I made my first Communion. I
will come to the world's end with you; but oh,
Sebastian, do not ask me, let me go. You will
forget me, I am a little girl to you, Sebastian.
You cannot care very much for me.'

The man looked down at her, smiling master-
fully, but very kindly. He took the mutinous
hand, with its little sprig of heather, and held it
between his own. He seemed to find her insistence adorable; mentally, he was contrasting

her with all other women whom he had known, frowning at the memory of so many years in which she had no part. He was a man of more than forty, built large to an uniform English pattern; there was a touch of military erectness in his carriage which often deceived people as to his vocation. Actually, he had never been anything but artist, though he came of a family of soldiers, and had once been war correspondent of an illustrated paper. A certain distinction had always adhered to him, never more than now when he was no longer young, was growing bald, had streaks of gray in his moustache. His face, without being handsome, possessed a certain charm; it was worn and rather pale, the lines about the firm mouth were full of lassitude, the eyes rather tired. He had the air of having tasted widely, curiously, of life in his day, prosperous as he seemed now, that had left its mark upon him. His voice, which usually took an intonation that his friends found supercilious, grew very tender in addressing this little French girl, with her quaint air of childish dignity.

'Marie-Yvonne, foolish child, I will not hear one word more. You are a little heretic; and I am sorely tempted to seal your lips from uttering heresy. You tell me that you love me, and

you ask me to let you go, in one breath. The
impossible conjuncture! Marie-Yvonne,' he
added, more seriously, 'trust yourself to me, my
child! You know, I will never give you up.
You know that these months that I have been
at Ploumariel, are worth all the rest of my life
to me. It has been a difficult life, hitherto,
little one : change it for me; make it worth while.
You would let morbid fancies come between us.
You have lived overmuch in that little church,
with its worm-eaten benches, and its mildewed
odour of dead people, and dead ideas. Take care,
Marie-Yvonne : it has made you serious-eyed,
before you have learnt to laugh ; by and by, it
will steal away your youth, before you have ever
been young. I come to claim you, Marie-
Yvonne, in the name of Life.' His words were
half-jesting ; his eyes were profoundly in earnest.
He drew her to him gently; and when he bent
down and kissed her forehead, and then her shy
lips, she made no resistance : only, a little tremor
ran through her. Presently, with equal gentleness, he put her away from him. 'You have
already given me your answer, Marie-Yvonne.
Believe me, you will never regret it. Let us go
down.'

They took their way in silence towards the

village; presently a bend of the road hid them from it, and he drew closer to her, helping her with his arm over the rough stones. Emerging, they had gone thirty yards so, before the scent of English tobacco drew their attention to a figure seated by the road-side, under a hedge; they recognised it, and started apart, a little consciously.

'It is M. Tregellan,' said the young girl, flushing : 'and he must have seen us.'

Her companion, frowning, hardly suppressed a little quick objurgation.

'It makes no matter,' he observed, after a moment : 'I shall see your uncle to-morrow and we know, good man, how he wishes this; and, in any case, I would have told Tregellan.'

The figure rose, as they drew near : he shook the ashes out of his briar, and removed it to his pocket. He was a slight man, with an ugly, clever face; his voice as he greeted them, was very low and pleasant.

'You must have had a charming walk, Mademoiselle. I have seldom seen Ploumariel look better.'

'Yes,' she said, gravely, 'it has been very pleasant. But I must not linger now,' she added breaking a little silence in which none of them

C

seemed quite at ease. ' My uncle will be expecting me to supper. She held out her hand, in the English fashion, to Tregellan, and then to Sebastian Murch; who gave the little fingers a private pressure.

They had come into the market-place round which most of the houses in Ploumariel were grouped. They watched the young girl cross it briskly; saw her blue gown pass out of sight down a bye street: then they turned to their own hotel. It was a low, white house, belted half way down the front with black stone; a pictorial object, as most Breton hostels. The ground floor was a *café;* and, outside it, a bench and long stained table enticed them to rest. They sat down, and ordered *absinthes*, as the hour suggested: these were brought to them presently by an old servant of the house; an admirable figure, with the white sleeves and apron relieving her linsey dress : with her good Breton face, and its effective wrinkles. For some time they sat in silence, drinking and smoking. The artist appeared to be absorbed in contemplation of his drink; considering its clouded green in various lights, After a while the other looked up, and remarked, abruptly.

'I may as well tell you that I happened to overlook you, just now, unintentionally.'

Sebastian Murch held up his glass, with absent eyes.

'Don't mention it, my dear fellow,' he remarked, at last, urbanely.

'I beg your pardon; but I am afraid I must.'

He spoke with an extreme deliberation which suggested nervousness; with the air of a person reciting a little set speech, learnt imperfectly: and he looked very straight in front of him, out into the street, at two dogs quarrelling over some offal.

'I daresay you will be angry: I can't avoid that; at least, I have known you long enough to hazard it. I have had it on my mind to say something. If I have been silent, it hasn't been because I have been blind, or approved. I have seen how it was all along. I gathered it from your letters when I was in England. Only until this afternoon I did not know how far it had gone, and now I am sorry I did not speak before.'

He stopped short, as though he expected his friend's subtilty to come to his assistance; with admissions or recriminations. But the other was still silent, absent: his face wore a look of

annoyed indifference. After a while, as Tregellan still halted, he observed quietly:

'You must be a little more explicit. I confess
I miss your meaning.'

'Ah, don't be paltry,' cried the other, quickly.
'You know my meaning. To be very plain,
Sebastian, are you quite justified in playing with
that charming girl, in compromising her?'

The artist looked up at last, smiling; his ex-
pressive mouth was set, not angrily, but with
singular determination.

'With Mademoiselle Mitouard?'

'Exactly; with the niece of a man whose
guest you have recently been.'

'My dear fellow!' he stopped a little, considering his words: 'You are hasty and unchar-
itable for such a very moral person! you jump
at conclusions, Tregellan. I don't, you know,
admit your right to question me: still, as you
have introduced the subject, I may as well
satisfy you. I have asked Mademoiselle Mitouard
to marry me, and she has consented, subject to
her uncle's approval. And that her uncle, who
happens to prefer the English method of court-
ship, is not likely to refuse.'

The other held his cigar between two fingers,
a little away; his curiously anxious face suggested

that the question had become to him one of increased nicety.

'I am sorry,' he said, after a moment; 'this is worse than I imagined; it's impossible.'

'It is you that are impossible, Tregellan,' said Sebastian Murch. He looked at him now, quite frankly, absolutely: his eyes had a defiant light in them, as though he hoped to be criticised; wished nothing better than to stand on his defence, to argue the thing out. And Tregellan sat for a long time without speaking, appreciating his purpose. It seemed more monstrous the closer he considered it: natural enough withal, and so, harder to defeat; and yet, he was sure, that defeated it must be. He reflected how accidental it had all been: their presence there, in Ploumariel, and the rest! Touring in Brittany, as they had often done before, in their habit of old friends, they had fallen upon it by chance, a place unknown of Murray; and the merest chance had held them there. They had slept at the *Lion d'Or*, voted it magnificently picturesque, and would have gone away and forgotten it; but the chance of travel had for once defeated them. Hard by they heard of the little votive chapel of Saint Bernard; at the suggestion of their hostess they set off to

visit it.   It was built steeply on an edge of rock,
amongst odorous pines overhanging a ravine, at
the bottom of which they could discern a brown
torrent purling tumidly along.   For the con-
venience of devotees, iron rings, at short intervals, were driven into the wall; holding
desperately to these, the pious pilgrim, at some
peril, might compass the circuit; saying an
oraison to Saint Bernard, and some ten *Aves*.
Sebastian, who was charmed with the wild
beauty of the scene, in a country ordinarily so
placid, had been seized with a fit of emulation :
not in any mood of devotion, but for the sake
of a wider prospect.   Tregellan had protested :
and the Saint, resenting the purely æsthetic
motive of the feat, had seemed to intervene.
For, half-way round, growing giddy may be, the
artist had made a false step, lost his hold.
Tregellan, with a little cry of horror, saw him
disappear amidst crumbling mortar and uprooted
ferns.   It was with a sensible relief, for the fall
had the illusion of great depth, that, making his
way rapidly down a winding path, he found him
lying on a grass terrace, amidst *débris* twenty
feet lower, cursing his folly, and holding a
lamentably sprained ankle, but for the rest un-
injured !   Tregellan had made off in haste to

Ploumariel in search of assistance; and within the hour he had returned with two stalwart Bretons and M. le Docteur Mitouard.

Their tour had been, naturally, drawing to its close. Tregellan indeed had an imperative need to be in London within the week. It seemed, therefore, a clear dispensation of Providence, that the amiable doctor should prove an hospitable person, and one inspiring confidence no less. Caring greatly for things foreign, and with an especial passion for England, a country whence his brother had brought back a wife; M. le Docteur Mitouard insisted that the invalid could be cared for properly at his house alone. And there, in spite of protestations, earnest from Sebastian, from Tregellan half-hearted, he was installed. And there, two days later, Tregellan left him with an easy mind; bearing away with him, half enviously, the recollection of the young, charming face of a girl, the Doctor's niece, as he had seen her standing by his friend's sofa when he paid his *adieux;* in the beginnings of an intimacy, in which, as he foresaw, the petulance of the invalid, his impatience at an enforced detention, might be considerably forgot. And all that had been two months ago.

II

'I am sorry you don't see it,' continued Tregellan, after a pause, 'to me it seems impossible;
considering your history it takes me by surprise.'

The other frowned slightly; finding this per-
sistence perhaps a trifle crude, he remarked good-
humouredly enough :

'Will you be good enough to explain your
opposition? Do you object to the girl? You
have been back a week now, during which you
have seen almost as much of her as I.'

'She is a child, to begin with; there is five-
and-twenty years' disparity between you. But
it's the relation I object to, not the girl. Do
you intend to live in Ploumariel?'

Sebastian smiled, with a suggestion of irony.

'Not precisely; I think it would interfere a
little with my career; why do you ask?'

'I imagined not; you will go back to London
with your little Breton wife, who is as charming
here as the apple-blossom in her own garden.
You will introduce her to your circle, who will
receive her with open arms; all the clever bores,
who write, and talk, and paint, and are talked
about between Bloomsbury and Kensington.

Everybody who is emancipated will know her, and everybody who has a "fad"; and they will come in a body and emancipate her, and teach her their "fads."'

'That is a caricature of my circle, as you call it, Tregellan! though I may remind you it is also yours. I think she is being starved in this corner, spiritually. She has a beautiful soul, and it has had no chance. I propose to give it one, and I am not afraid of the result.'

Tregellan threw away the stump of his cigar into the darkling street, with a little gesture of discouragement, of lassitude.

'She has had the chance to become what she is, a perfect thing.'

'My dear fellow,' exclaimed his friend, 'I could not have said more myself.'

The other continued, ignoring his interruption.

'She has had great luck. She has been brought up by an old eccentric, on the English system of growing up as she liked. And no harm has come of it, at least until it gave you the occasion of making love to her.'

'You are candid, Tregellan!'

'Let her go, Sebastian, let her go,' he continued, with increasing gravity. 'Consider what a transplantation; from this world of Ploumariel

where everything is fixed for her by that vener-
able old *Curé*, where life is so easy, so ordered,
to yours, ours; a world without definitions,
where everything is an open question.'

' Exactly,' said the artist, ' why should she be
so limited? I would give her scope, ideas. I
can't see that I am wrong.'

'She will not accept them, your ideas. They
will trouble her, terrify her; in the end, divide
you. It is not an elastic nature. I have watched
it.'

' At least, allow me to know her,' put in the
artist, a little grimly.

Tregellan shook his head.

'The Breton blood; her English mother:
passionate Catholicism! a touch of Puritan!
Have you quite made up your mind, Sebastian?'

' I made it up long ago, Tregellan!'

The other looked at him, curiously, compas-
sionately; with a touch of resentment at what
he found his lack of subtilty. Then he said at
last :

'I called it impossible : you force me to be
very explicit, even cruel. I must remind you,
that you are, of all my friends, the one I value
most, could least afford to lose.'

' You must be going to say something extremely disagreeable! something horrible,' said the artist, slowly.

'I am,' said Tregellan, 'but I must say it. Have you explained to Mademoiselle, or her uncle, your—your peculiar position?'

Sebastian was silent for a moment, frowning: the lines about his mouth grew a little sterner; at last he said coldly:

'If I were to answer, Yes?'

'Then I should understand that there was no further question of your marriage.'

Presently the other commenced in a hard, leaden voice.

'No, I have not told Marie-Yvonne that. I shall not tell her. I have suffered enough for a youthful folly; an act of mad generosity. I refuse to allow an infamous woman to wreck my future life as she has disgraced my past. Legally, she has passed out of it; morally, legally, she is not my wife. For all I know she may be actually dead.'

The other was watching his face, very gray and old now, with an anxious compassion.

'You know she is not dead, Sebastian,' he said simply. Then he added very quietly as one breaks supreme bad tidings, 'I must tell you something which I fear you have not realised.

The Catholic Church does not recognise divorce.
If she marry you and find out, rightly or wrongly
she will believe that she has been living in sin;
some day she will find it out. No damnable
secret like that keeps itself for ever: an old
newspaper, a chance remark from one of your
dear friends, and, the deluge. Do you see the
tragedy, the misery of it? By God, Sebastian,
to save you both somebody shall tell her; and if
it be not you, it must be I.'

There was extremest peace in the quiet square;
the houses seemed sleepy at last, after a day of
exhausting tranquillity, and the chestnuts, under
which a few children, with tangled hair and fair
dirty faces, still played. The last glow of the
sun fell on the gray roofs opposite; dying hard
it seemed over the street in which the Mitouards
lived; and they heard suddenly the tinkle of an
Angelus bell. Very placid! the place and the
few peasants in their pictorial hats and caps who
lingered. Only the two Englishmen sitting,
their glasses empty, and their smoking over,
looking out on it all with their anxious faces,
brought in a contrasting note of modern life; of
the complex aching life of cities, with its troubles
and its difficulties.

'Is that your final word, Tregellan?' asked the artist at last, a little wearily.

'It must be, Sebastian! Believe me, I am infinitely sorry.'

'Yes, of course,' he answered quickly, acidly; 'well, I will sleep on it.'

III

They made their first breakfast in an almost total silence; both wore the bruised harassed air which tells of a night passed without benefit of sleep. Immediately afterwards Murch went out alone: Tregellan could guess the direction of his visit, but not its object; he wondered if the artist was making his difficult confession. Presently they brought him in a pencilled note; he recognised, with some surprise, his friend's tortuous hand.

'I have considered our conversation, and your unjustifiable interference. I am entirely in your hands: at the mercy of your extraordinary notions of duty. Tell her what you will, if you must; and pave the way to your own success. I shall say nothing; but I swear you love the girl yourself; and are no right arbiter here. Sebastian Murch.'

He read the note through twice before he grasped its purport; then sat holding it in lax fingers, his face grown singularly gray.

'It's not true, it's not true,' he cried aloud, but a moment later knew himself for a self-deceiver all along. Never had self-consciousness been more sudden, unexpected, or complete. There was no more to do or say; this knowledge tied his hands. *Ite! missa est!* . . .

He spent an hour painfully invoking casuistry, tossed to and fro irresolutely, but never for a moment disputing that plain fact which Sebastian had so brutally illuminated. Yes! he loved her, had loved her all along. Marie-Yvonne! how the name expressed her! at once sweet and serious, arch and sad as her nature. The little Breton wild flower! how cruel it seemed to gather her! And he could do no more; Sebastian had tied his hands. Things must be! He was a man nicely conscientious, and now all the elaborate devices of his honour, which had persuaded him to a disagreeable interference, were contraposed against him. This suspicion of an ulterior motive had altered it, and so at last he was left to decide with a sigh, that because he loved these two so well, he must let them go their own way to misery.

Coming in later in the day, Sebastian Murch found his friend packing.

'I have come to get your answer,' he said; 'I have been walking about the hills like a madman for hours. I have not been near her; I am afraid. Tell me what you mean to do ?'

Tregellan rose, shrugged his shoulders, pointed to his valise.

'God help you both ! I would have saved you if you had let me. The Quimperlé *Courrier* passes in half-an-hour. I am going by it. I shall catch a night train to Paris.'

As Sebastian said nothing; continued to regard him with the same dull, anxious gaze, he went on after a moment :

'You did me a grave injustice; you should have known me better than that. God knows I meant nothing shameful, only the best; the least misery for you and her.'

'It was true then ?' said Sebastian, curiously. His voice was very cold; Tregellan found him altered. He regarded the thing as it had been very remote, and outside them both.

'I did not know it then,' said Tregellan, shortly.

He knelt down again and resumed his packing. Sebastian, leaning against the bed, watched him with absent intensity, which was yet alive to trivial things, and he handed him from time to time a book, a brush, which the other packed mechanically with elaborate care. There was no more to say, and presently, when the chamber-maid entered for his luggage, they went down and out into the splendid sunshine, silently. They had to cross the Square to reach the carriage, a dusty ancient vehicle, hooded, with places for four, which waited outside the post-office. A man in a blue blouse preceded them, carrying Tregellan's things. From the corner they could look down the road to Quimperlé, and their eyes both sought the white house of Doctor Mitouard, standing back a little in its trim garden, with its one incongruous apple tree; but there was no one visible.

Presently, Sebastian asked, suddenly :

' Is it true, that you said last night : divorce to a Catholic—? '

Tregellan interrupted him.

' It is absolutely true, my poor friend.'

He had climbed into his place at the back, settled himself on the shiny leather cushion : he appeared to be the only passenger. Sebastian stood looking drearily in at the window, the glass of which had long perished.

'I wish I had never known, Tregellan! How could I ever tell her!'

Inside, Tregellan shrugged his shoulders : not impatiently, or angrily, but in sheer impotence; as one who gave it up.

'I can't help you,' he said, 'you must arrange it with your own conscience.'

'Ah, it's too difficult!' cried the other : 'I can't find my way.'

The driver cracked his whip, suggestively; Sebastian drew back a little further from the off wheel.

'Well,' said the other, 'if you find it, write and tell me. I am very sorry, Sebastian.'

'Good-bye,' he replied. 'Yes! I will write.'

The carriage lumbered off, with a lurch to the right, as it turned the corner ; it rattled down the hill, raising a cloud of white dust. As it passed the Mitouards' house, a young girl, in a large straw hat, came down the garden; too late to discover whom it contained. She watched it out of sight, indifferently, leaning on the little iron gate ; then she turned, to recognise the long stooping figure of Sebastian Murch, who advanced to meet her.

D

AN ORCHESTRAL VIOLIN

I

At my dining-place in old Soho—I call it mine because there was a time when I became somewhat inveterate there, keeping my napkin (changed once a week) in a ring recognisable by myself and the waiter, my bottle of Beaune (replenished more frequently), and my accustomed seat—at this restaurant of mine, with its confusion of tongues, its various, foreign *clientèle*, amid all the coming and going, the nightly change of faces, there were some which remained the same, persons with whom, though one might never have spoken, one had nevertheless from the mere continuity of juxtaposition a certain sense of intimacy.

There was one old gentleman in particular, as inveterate as myself, who especially aroused my interest. A courteous, punctual, mild old man

with an air which deprecated notice; who con-
versed each evening for a minute or two with
the proprietor, as he rolled, always at the same
hour, a valedictory cigarette, in a language that
arrested my ear by its strangeness; and which
proved to be his own, Hungarian; who addressed
a brief remark to me at times, half apologetically,
in the precisest of English. We sat next each
other at the same table, came and went at much
the same hour; and for a long while our inter-
course was restricted to formal courtesies; mutual
inquiries after each other's health, a few urbane
strictures on the climate. The little old gentleman in spite of his aspect of shabby gentility,—
for his coat was sadly inefficient, and the nap of
his carefully brushed hat did not indicate prosperity—perhaps even because of this suggestion
of fallen fortunes, bore himself with pathetic
erectness, almost haughtily. He did not seem
amenable to advances. It was a long time before
I knew him well enough to value rightly this
appearance, the timid defences, behind which a
very shy and delicate nature took refuge from
the world's coarse curiosity. I can smile now,
with a certain sadness, when I remind myself
that at one time I was somewhat in awe of
M. Maurice Cristich and his little air of proud

humility. Now that his place in that dim, foreign eating-house knows him no more, and his yellow napkin-ring, with its distinguishing number, has been passed on to some other customer; I have it in my mind to set down my impressions of him, the short history of our acquaintance. It began with an exchange of cards; a form to which he evidently attached a ceremonial value, for after that piece of ritual his manner underwent a sensible softening, and he showed by many subtile indefinable shades in his courteous address, that he did me the honour of including me in his friendship. I have his card before me now; a large, oblong piece of pasteboard, with *M. Maurice Cristich, Theatre Royal*, inscribed upon it, amid many florid flourishes. It enabled me to form my first definite notion of his calling, upon which I had previously wasted much conjecture; though I had all along, and rightly as it appeared, associated him in some manner with music.

In time he was good enough to inform me further. He was a musician, a violinist; and formerly, and in his own country, he had been a composer. But whether for some lack in him of original talent, or of patience, whether for some grossness in the public taste, on which the ner-

vous delicacy and refinement of his execution
was lost, he had not continued. He had been
driven by poverty to London, had given lessons,
and then for many years had played a second
violin in the orchestra of the Opera.

'It is not much, Monsieur!' he observed, de-
precatingly, smoothing his hat with the cuff of
his frayed coat-sleeve. 'But it is sufficient; and
I prefer it to teaching. In effect, they are very
charming, the seraphic young girls of your
country! But they seem to care little for music;
and I am a difficult master, and have not enough
patience. Once, you see, a long time ago, I had
a perfect pupil, and perhaps that spoilt me. Yes!
I prefer the theatre, though it is less profitable.
It is not as it once was,' he added, with a half
sigh; 'I am no longer ambitious. Yes, Monsieur,
when I was young, I was ambitious. I wrote a
symphony and several concertos. I even brought
out at Vienna an opera, which I thought would
make me famous; but the good folk of Vienna
did not appreciate me, and they would have
none of my music. They said it was antiquated,
my opera, and absurd; and yet, it seemed to me
good. I think that Gluck, that great genius,
would have liked it; and that is what I should
have wished. Ah! how long ago it seems, that

time when I was ambitious! But you must
excuse me, Monsieur! your good company
makes me garrulous. I must be at the theatre.
If I am not in my place at the half-hour, they
fine me two shillings and sixpence, and that
I can ill afford, you know, Monsieur!'

In spite of his defeats, his long and ineffectual
struggle with adversity, M. Cristich, I discovered,
as our acquaintance ripened, had none of the
spleen and little of the vanity of the unsuccessful
artist. He seemed in his forlorn old age to have
accepted his discomfiture with touching resig-
nation, having acquired neither cynicism nor
indifference. He was simply an innocent old
man, in love with his violin and with his art,
who had acquiesced in disappointment; and it
was impossible to decide, whether he even believed in his talent, or had not silently accredited
the verdict of musical Vienna, which had con-
demned his opera in those days when he was
ambitious. The precariousness of the London
Opera was the one fact which I ever knew to
excite him to expressions of personal resentment.
When its doors were closed, his hard poverty (it
was the only occasion when he protested against
it), drove him, with his dear instrument and his
accomplished fingers, into the orchestras of lighter

houses, where he was compelled to play music which he despised. He grew silent and rueful during these periods of irksome servitude, rolled innumerable cigarettes, which he smoked with fierceness and great rapidity. When dinner was done, he was often volubly indignant, in Hungarian, to the proprietor. But with the beginning of the season his mood lightened. He bore himself more sprucely, and would leave me, to assist at a representation of *Don Giovanni*, or *Tannhauser*, with a face which was almost radiant. I had known him a year before it struck me that I should like to see him in his professional capacity. I told him of my desire a little diffidently, not knowing how my purpose might strike him. He responded graciously, but with an air of intrigue, laying a gentle hand upon my coat sleeve and bidding me wait. A day or two later, as we sat over our coffee, M. Cristich with an hesitating urbanity offered me an order.

'If you would do me the honour to accept it, Monsieur! It is a stall, and a good one! I have never asked for one before, all these years, so they gave it to me easily. You see, I have few friends. It is for to-morrow, as you observe, I demanded it especially; it is an occasion of

great interest to me,—ah! an occasion! You
will come?'

'You are too good, M. Cristich!' I said with
genuine gratitude, for indeed the gift came in
season, the opera being at that time a luxury I
could seldom command. 'Need I say that I
shall be delighted? And to hear Madame
Romanoff, a chance one has so seldom!'

The old gentleman's mild, dull eyes glistened.
'Madame Romanoff!' he repeated, 'the marvellous Leonora! yes, yes! She has sung only
once before in London. Ah, when I remember
—' He broke off suddenly. As he rose, and
prepared for departure, he held my hand a little
longer than usual, giving it a more intimate
pressure.

'My dear young friend, will you think me a
presumptuous old man, if I ask you to come and
see me to-morrow in my apartment, when it is
over? I will give you a glass of whisky, and
we will smoke pipes, and you shall tell me your
impressions—and then I will tell you why to-
morrow I shall be so proud, why I show this
emotion.'

II

THE Opera was *Fidelio*, that stately, splendid
work, whose melody, if one may make a pictorial
comparison, has something of that rich and sun-
warm colour which, certainly, on the canvasses
of Rubens, affects one as an almost musical
quality. It offered brilliant opportunities, and
the incomparable singer had wasted none of
them. So that when, at last, I pushed my way
out of the crowded house and joined M. Cristich
at the stage door, where he waited with eyes full
of expectancy, the music still lingered about me,
like the faint, past fragrance of incense, and I
had no need to speak my thanks. He rested a
light hand on my arm, and we walked towards
his lodging silently; the musician carrying his
instrument in its sombre case, and shivering
from time to time, a tribute to the keen spring
night. He stooped as he walked, his eyes trail-
ing the ground; and a certain listlessness in his
manner struck me a little strangely, as though
he came fresh from some solemn or hieratic
experience, of which the reaction had already
begun to set in tediously, leaving him at the
last unstrung and jaded, a little weary, of himself

and the too strenuous occasion. It was not until we had crossed the threshold of a dingy, high house in a byway of Bloomsbury, and he had ushered me, with apologies, into his shabby room, near the sky, that the sense of his hospitable duties seemed to renovate him.

He produced tumblers from an obscure recess behind his bed; set a kettle on the fire, a lodging-house fire, which scarcely smouldered with flickers of depressing, sulphurous flame, talking of indifferent subjects, as he watched for it to boil.

Only when we had settled ourselves, in uneasy chairs, opposite each other, and he had composed me, what he termed 'a grog': himself preferring the more innocent mixture known as *eau sucrée*, did he allude to *Fidelio*. I praised heartily the discipline of the orchestra, the prima donna, whom report made his country-woman, with her strong, sweet voice and her extraordinary beauty, the magnificence of the music, the fine impression of the whole.

M. Cristich, his glass in hand, nodded approval. He looked intently into the fire, which cast mocking shadows over his quaint, incongruous figure, his antiquated dress coat, which seemed to skimp him, his frost-bitten countenance, his

cropped gray hair. 'Yes,' he said, 'Yes! So it
pleased you, and you thought her beautiful? I
am glad.'

He turned round to me abruptly, and laid a
thin hand impressively on my knee.

'You know I invented her, the Romanoff,
discovered her, taught her all she learnt. Yes,
Monsieur, I was proud to-night, very proud, to
be there, playing for her, though she did not
know. Ah! the beautiful creature! . . . . and
how badly I played! execrably! You could not
notice that, Monsieur, but they did, my *confrères,*
and could not understand. How should they?
How should they dream, that I, Maurice Cristich,
second violin in the orchestra of the opera, had
to do with the Leonora; even I! Her voice
thrilled them; ah, but it was I who taught her
her notes! They praised her diamonds; yes,
but once I gave her that she wanted more than
diamonds, bread, and lodging and love. Beautiful they called her; she was beautiful too, when
I carried her in my arms through Vienna. I am
an old man now, and good for very little; and
there have been days, God forgive me! when I
have been angry with her; but it was not to-
night. To see her there, so beautiful and so
great; and to feel that after all I had a hand in

it, that I invented her. Yes, yes! I had my victory to-night too ; though it was so private ; a secret between you and me, Monsieur? Is it not ? '

I assured him of my discretion, but he hardly seemed to hear. His sad eyes had wandered away to the live coals, and he considered them pensively, as though he found them full of charming memories. I sat back, respecting his remoteness; but my silence was replete with surprised conjecture, and indeed the quaint figure of the old musician, every line of his garments redolent of ill success, had become to me, of a sudden, strangely romantic. Destiny, so amorous of surprises, of pathetic or cynical contrasts, had in this instance excelled herself. My obscure acquaintance, Maurice Cristich! The renowned Romanoff! Her name and acknowledged genius had been often in men's mouths of late, a certain luminous, scarcely sacred, glamour attaching to it, in an hundred idle stories, due perhaps as much to the wonder of her sorrowful beauty, as to any justification in knowledge, of her boundless extravagance, her magnificent fantasies, her various perversity, rumour pointing specially at those priceless diamonds, the favours not altogether gratuitous

it was said of exalted personages. And with all
deductions made, for malice, for the ingenuity of
the curious, the impression of her perversity was
left; she remained enigmatical and notorious, a
somewhat scandalous heroine! And Cristich
had known her; he had, as he declared, and his
accent was not that of bragadoccio, invented her.
The conjuncture puzzled and fascinated me. It
did not make Cristich less interesting, nor the
prima-donna more perspicuous.

By-and-by the violinist looked up at me; he
smiled with a little dazed air, as though his
thoughts had been a far journey.

'Pardon me, Monsieur! I beg you to fill
your glass. I seem a poor host; but to tell you
the truth, I was dreaming; I was quite away,
quite away.'

He threw out his hands, with a vague ex-
pansive gesture.

'Dear child!' he said to the flames, in French;
'good little one! I do not forget thee.' And he
began to tell me.

'It was when I was at Vienna, ah! a long
while ago. I was not rich, but neither was I
very poor; I still had my little patrimony, and
I lived in the ——— Strasse, very economically;
it is a quarter which many artists frequent. I

husbanded my resources, that I might be able
to work away at my art without the tedium
of making it a means of livelihood. ˙I refused
many offers to play in public, that I might have
more leisure. I should not do that now; but
then, I was very confident; I had great faith in
me. And I worked very hard at my symphony,
and I was full of desire to write an opera. It
was a tall dark house, where I lived; there were
many other lodgers, but I knew scarcely any of
them. I went about with my head full of music
and I had my violin; I had no time to seek
acquaintance. Only my neighbour, at the other
side of my passage, I knew slightly and bowed
to him when we met on the stairs. He was a
dark, lean man, of a very distinguished air; he
must have lived very hard, he had death in his
face. He was not an artist, like the rest of us:
I suspect he was a great profligate, and a
gambler; but he had the manners of a gentleman. And when I came to talk to him, he
displayed the greatest knowledge of music that
I have ever known. And it was the same with
all; he talked divinely, of everything in the
world, but very wildly and bitterly. He seemed
to have been everywhere, and done everything;
and at last to be tired of it all; and of himself

E

the most. From the people of the house I
heard that he was a Pole; noble, and very poor;
and, what surprised me, that he had a daughter
with him, a little girl. I used to pity this child,
who must have lived quite alone. For the
Count was always out, and the child never
appeared with him; and, for the rest, with his
black spleen and tempers, he must have been
but sorry company for a little girl. I wished
much to see her; for you see, Monsieur! I am
fond of children, almost as much as of music;
and one day it came about. I was at home with
my violin; I had been playing all the evening
some songs I had made; and once or twice I
had seemed to be interrupted by little, tedious
sounds. At last I stopped, and opened the door;
and there, crouching down, I found the most
beautiful little creature I had ever seen in my
life. It was the child of my neighbour. Yes,
Monsieur! you divine, you divine! That was
the Leonora!'

'And she is not your compatriot,' I asked.

'A Hungarian? ah, no! yet every piece of her
pure Slav. But I weary you, Monsieur; I make
a long story.'

I protested my interest; and after a little side
glance of dubious scrutiny, he continued in a

constrained monotone, as one who told over to himself some rosary of sad enchanting memories.

'Ah, yes! she was beautiful; that mysterious, sad Slavonic beauty! a thing quite special and apart. And, as a child, it was more tragical and strange; that dusky hair! those profound and luminous eyes! seeming to mourn over tragedies they have never known. A strange, wild, silent child! She might have been eight or nine, then; but her little soul was hungry for music. It was a veritable passion; and when she became at last my good friend, she told me how often she had lain for long hours outside my door, listening to my violin. I gave her a kind of scolding, such as one could to so beautiful a little creature, for the passage was draughty and cold, and sent her away with some *bon-bons*. She shook back her long, dark hair: 'You are not angry, and I am not naughty,' she said: 'and I shall come back. I thank you for your *bon-bons*; but I like your music better than *bon-bons*, or fairy tales, or anything in the world.'

But she never came back to the passage again, Monsieur! The next time I came across the Count, I sent her an invitation, a little diffidently, for he had never spoken to me of her, and he was a strange and difficult man. Now, he simply shrugged his shoulders, with a smile, in which, for once, there seemed more entertainment than malice. The child could visit me when she chose ; if it amused either of us, so much the better. And we were content, and she came to me often ; after a while, indeed, she was with me almost always. Child as she was, she had already the promise of her magnificent voice ; and I taught her to use it, to sing, and to play on the piano and on the violin, to which she took the most readily. She was like a singing bird in the room, such pure, clear notes ! And she grew very fond of me ; she would fall asleep at last in my arms, and so stay until the Count would take her with him when he entered, long after midnight. He came to me naturally for her soon ; and they never seemed long those hours that I watched over her sleep. I never knew him harsh or unkind to the child ; he seemed simply indifferent to her as to everything else. He had exhausted life and he hated it ; and he knew that death was on him, and he hated that even more. And yet he was careful of her after a fashion, buying her *bon-bons* and little costumes, when he was in the vein, pitching his voice softly when he would stay and talk to me, as though he relished her sleep. One night he did not come to fetch her at all, I had wrapped a blanket round the child where she lay on my bed, and had sat down to watch by her and presently I too fell asleep. I do not know how long I slept but when I woke there was a gray light in the room, I was very cold and stiff, but I could hear close by, the soft, regular breathing of the child. There was a great uneasiness on me, and after a while I stole out across the passage and knocked at the Count's door, there was no answer but it gave when I tried it, and so I went in. The lamp had smouldered out, there was a sick odour of *pétrol* everywhere, and the shutters were closed: but through the chinks the merciless gray dawn streamed in and showed me the Count sitting very still by the table. His face wore a most curious smile, and had not his great cavernous eyes been open, I should have believed him asleep: suddenly it came to me that he was dead. He was not a good man, monsieur, nor an amiable, but a true *virtuoso* and full of information, and I grieved. I have had Masses said for the repose of his soul,'

He paid a tribute of silence to the dead man's memory, and then he went on.

'It seemed quite natural that I should take his child. There was no one to care, no one to object; it happened quite easily. We went, the little one and I, to another part of the city. We made quite a new life. Oh! my God! it is a very long time ago.'

Quite suddenly his voice went tremulous; but after a pause, hardly perceptible, he recovered himself and continued with an accent of apology.

'I am a foolish old man, and very garrulous. It is not good to think of that, nor to talk of it; I do not know why I do. But what would you have? She loved me then, and she had the voice and the disposition of an angel. I have never been very happy. I think sometimes, monsieur, that we others, who care much for art, are not permitted that. But certainly those few, rapid days, when she was a child, were good; and yet they were the days of my defeat. I found myself out then. I was never to be a great artist, a *maestro:* a second-rate man, a good music-teacher for young ladies, a capable performer in an orchestra, what you will, but a great artist, never! Yet in those days, even when my opera failed, I had consolation, I could say, I have a child! I would have kept her with me always but it could not be, from the very first she would be a singer. I knew always that a day would come when she would not need me,

she was meant to be the world's delight, and I
had no right to keep her, even if I could.   I held
my beautiful, strange bird in her cage, until she
beat her wings against the bars, then I opened
the door.   At the last, I think, that is all we can
do for our children, our best beloved, our very
heart-strings, stand free of them, let them go.
The world is very weary, but we must all find
that out for ourselves, perhaps when they are
tired they will come home, perhaps not, perhaps
not.   It was to the Conservatoire, at Milan, that
I sent her finally, and it was at La Scala that she
afterwards appeared, and at La Scala too, poor
child, she met her evil genius, the man named
Romanoff, a baritone in her company, own son
of the devil, whom she married.   Ah, if I could
have prevented it, if I could have prevented it !'

He lapsed into a long silence; a great weariness
seemed to have come over him, and in the gray
light which filtered in through the dingy window
blinds, his face was pinched and wasted, unutter-
ably old and forlorn.

'But I did not prevent it,' he said at last, ' for
all my good will, perhaps merely hastened it by
unseasonable interference.   And so we went in
different ways, with anger I fear, and at least
with sore hearts and misunderstanding.'

He spoke with an accent of finality, and so sadly that in a sudden rush of pity I was moved to protest.

'But, surely you meet sometimes; surely this woman, who was as your own child—'

He stopped me with a solemn, appealing gesture.

'You are young, and you do not altogether understand. You must not judge her; you must not believe, that she forgets, that she does not care. Only, it is better like this, because it could never be as before. I could not help her. I want nothing that she can give me, no not anything; I have my memories! I hear of her, from time to time; I hear what the world says of her, the imbecile world, and I smile. Do I not know best? I, who carried her in my arms, when she was that high!'

And in effect the old violinist smiled, it was as though he had surprised my secret of dissatisfaction, and found it, like the malice of the world, too ignorant to resent. The edge of his old, passionate adoration had remained bright and keen through the years; and it imparted a strange brilliancy to his eyes, which half convinced me, as presently, with a resumption of his usual air of diffident courtesy, he ushered me out into the vague, spring dawn. And yet, when I had parted from him and was making my way somewhat wearily to my own quarters, my first dubious impression remained. My imagination was busy with the story I had heard, striving quite vainly to supply omissions, to fill in meagre outlines. Yes! quite vainly! the figure of the Romanoff was left, ambiguous and un- explained; hardly acquitted in my mind of a certain callousness, an ingratitude almost vulgar as it started out from time to time, in contraposi- tion against that forlorn old age.

III

I saw him once more at the little restaurant in Soho, before a sudden change of fortune, calling me abroad for an absence, as it happened, of years, closed the habit of our society. He gave me the god-speed of a brother artist, though mine was not the way of music, with many prophesies of my success; and the pressure of his hand, as he took leave of me, was tremulous.

'I am an old man, monsieur, and we may not meet again, in this world. I wish you all the chances you deserve in Paris; but I—I shall greatly miss you. If you come back in time, you will find me in the old places; and if not— there are things of mine, which I should wish you to have, that shall be sent you.'

And indeed it proved to be our last meeting. I went to Paris; a fitful correspondence intervened, grew infrequent, ceased; then a little later, came to me the notification, very brief and official, of his death in the French Hospital of pneumonia. It was followed by a few remembrances of him, sent at his request, I learnt, by the priest who had administered to him the last offices : some books that he had greatly cherished, works of Glück, for the most part; an antique ivory crucifix of very curious workmanship; and his violin, a beautiful instrument dated 1670 and made at Nuremberg, yet with a tone which seemed to me, at least, as fine as that of the Cremonas. It had an intrinsic value to me, apart from its associations; for I too was something of an amateur, and since this seasoned melodious wood had come into my possession, I was inspired to take my facility more seriously. To play in public, indeed, I had neither leisure nor desire : but in certain *salons* of my acquaintance, where music was much in vogue, I made from time to time a desultory appearance. I set

down these facts, because as it happened, this
ineffectual talent of mine, which poor Cristich's
legacy had recalled to life, was to procure me
an interesting encounter. I remember the occasion well, it was too appropriate to be forgotten
—as though my old friend's lifeless fiddle, which
had yet survived so many *maestri*, was to be a
direct instrument of the completion of his story,
the resurrection of those dormant and unsatisfied
curiosities which still now and again concerned
me. I had played at an house where I was a
stranger ; brought there by a friend, to whose
insistence I had yielded somewhat reluctantly ;
although he had assured me, and, I believe, with
reason, that it was a house where the indirect, or
Attic invitation greatly prevailed, in brief, a place
where one met very queer people. The hostess
was American, a charming woman, of unimpeach-
able antecedents ; but her passion for society,
which, while it should always be interesting, was
not always equally reputable, had exposed her
evenings to the suspicion of her compatriots.
And when I had discharged my part in the
programme and had leisure to look around me, I
saw at a glance that their suspicion was justified;
very queer people indeed were there. The large
hot rooms were cosmopolitan: infidels and Jews,

everybody and nobody ; a scandalously promis-
cuous assemblage ! And there, with a half start,
which was not at first recognition, my eyes
stopped before a face which brought to me a confused rush of memories. It was that of a woman
who sat on an ottoman in the smallest room
which was almost empty. Her companion was
a small, vivacious man with a gray imperial,
and the red ribbon in his buttonhole, to whose
continuous stream of talk, eked out with meri-
dional gestures, she had the air of being listlessly
resigned. Her dress, a marvel of discretion,
its colour the yellow of old ivory, was of some
very rich and stiff stuff cut square to her neck ;
that, and her great black hair, clustered to a
crimson rose at the top of her head, made the
pallor of her face a thing to marvel at. Her
beauty was at once sombre and illuminating, and
youthful no less. The woman of thirty : but
her complexion, and her arms, which were bare,
were soft in texture as a young girl's.

I made my way as well as I could for the
crowd, to my hostess, listened, with what patience
I might, to some polite praise of my playing,
and made my request.

'Mrs Destrier, I have an immense favour to
ask ; introduce me to Madame Romanoff!'

She gave me a quick, shrewd smile ; then I remembered stories of her intimate quaintness.

'My dear young man ! I have no objection. Only I warn you, she is not conversational ; you will make no good of it, and you will be disappointed ; perhaps that will be best. Please remember, I am responsible for nobody.'

'Is she so dangerous ?' I asked. 'But never mind ; I believe that I have something to say which may interest her.'

'Oh, for that !' she smiled eliptically ; 'yes, she is most dangerous. But I will introduce you ; you shall tell me how you succeed.'

I bowed and smiled ; she laid a light hand on my arm ; and I piloted her to the desired corner. It seemed that the chance was with me. The little fluent Provençal had just vacated his seat ; and when the prima-donna had acknowledged the hasty mention of my name, with a bare inclination of her head, I was emboldened to succeed to it. And then I was silent. In the perfection of that dolorous face, I could not but be reminded of the tradition which has always ascribed something fatal and inevitable to the possession of great gifts: of genius or uncommon fortune, or singular personal beauty ; and the common-place of conversation failed me.

After a while she looked askance at me, with a sudden flash of resentment.

'You speak no French, Monsieur! And yet you write it well enough; I have read your stories.'

I acknowledged Madame's irony, permitted myself to hope that my efforts had met with Madame's approval.

'*A la bonne heure!* I perceive you also speak it. Is that why you wished to be presented, to hear my criticisms?'

'Let me answer that question when you have answered mine.'

She glanced curiously over her feathered fan, then with the slightest upward inclination of her statuesque shoulders—'I admire your books; but are your women quite just? I prefer your playing.'

'That is better, Madame! It was to talk of that I came.'

'Your playing?'

'My violin.'

'You want me to look at it? It is a Cremona?'

'It is not a Cremona; but if you like, I will give it you.'

Her dark eyes shone out in amazed amusement.

'You are eccentric, Monsieur! but your nation has a privilege of eccentricity. At least, you amuse me ; and I have wearied myself enough this long evening. Show me your violin ; I am something of a *virtuosa.*'

I took the instrument from its case, handed it to her in silence, watching her gravely. She received it with the dexterous hands of a musician, looked at the splendid stains on the back, then bent over towards the light in a curious scrutiny of the little, faded signature of its maker, the *fecit* of an obscure Bavarian of the seventeenth century ; and it was a long time before she raised her eyes.

When she spoke, her rich voice had a note of imperious entreaty in it. 'Your violin interests me, Monsieur! Oh, I know that wood! It came to you—?'

'A legacy from an esteemed friend.'

She shot back. 'His name?' with the flash which I waited for.

'Maurice Cristich, Madame!'

We were deserted in our corner. The company had strayed in, one by one, to the large *salon* with the great piano, where a young Russian musician, a pupil of Chopin, sat down to play, with no conventional essay of preliminary chords, an expected morsel. The strains of it wailed in just then, through the heavy, screening curtains ; a mad *valse* of his own, that no human feet could dance to, a pitiful, passionate thing that thrilled the nerves painfully, ringing the changes between voluptuous sorrow and the merriment of devils, and burdened always with the weariness of 'all the Russias,' the proper *Welt-schmerz* of a young, disconsolate people. It seemed to charge the air, like electricity, with passionate undertones ; it gave intimate facilities, and a tense personal note to our interview.

'A legacy ! so he is gone.' She swayed to me with a wail in her voice, in a sort of childish abandonment : 'and *you* tell me ! Ah !' she drew back, chilling suddenly with a touch of visible suspicion. 'You hurt me, Monsieur ! Is it a stroke at random ? You spoke of a gift ; you say you knew, esteemed him. You were with him ? Perhaps, a message . . . ?'

'He died alone, Madame ! I have no message. If there were none, it might be, perhaps, that he believed you had not cared for it. If that were wrong, I could tell you that you were not forgotten. Oh ! he loved you ! I had his word for it, and the story. The violin is yours—do not mistake me; it is not for your sake but his.

He died alone ; value it, as I should,
Madame ! '

They were insolent words, perhaps cruel, pro-
voked from me by the mixed nature of my
attraction to her; the need of turning a reasonable and cool front to that pathetic beauty, that
artful music, which whipped jaded nerves to
mutiny. The arrow in them struck so true, that
I was shocked at my work. It transfixed the
child in her, latent in most women, which
moaned at my feet; so that for sheer shame as
though it were actually a child I had hurt, I
could have fallen and kissed her hands.

'Oh, you judge me hard, you believe the
worst of me and why not ? I am against the
world ! At least he might have taught you to
be generous, that kind old man ! Have I forgotten do you think ! Am I so happy then ?
Oh it is a just question, the world busies itself
with me, and you are in the lap of its tongues.
Has it ever accused me of that, of happiness ?
Cruel, cruel ! I have paid my penalties, and a
woman is not free to do as she will, but would
not I have gone to him, for a word, a sign ?
Yes, for the sake of my childhood. And to-night
when you showed me that,' her white hand
swept over the violin with something of a caress,

F

'I thought it had come, yes, from the grave, and you make it more bitter by readings of your own. You strike me hard.'

I bent forward in real humility, her voice had tears in it, though her splendid eyes were hard.

'Forgive me, Madame! a vulgar stroke at random. I had no right to make it, he told me only good of you. Forgive me, and for proof of your pardon—I am serious now—take his violin.'

Her smile, as she refused me, was full of sad dignity.

'You have made it impossible, Monsieur! It would remind me only now of how ill you think of me. I beg you to keep it.'

The music had died away suddenly, and its ceasing had been followed by a loud murmur of applause. The prima-donna rose, and stood for a moment observing me, irresolutely.

'I leave you and your violin, Monsieur! I have to sing presently, with such voice as our talk has left me. I bid you both adieu!'

'Ah Madame!' I deprecated, 'you will think again of this, I will send it you in the morning. I have no right . . .'

She shook her head, then with a sudden flash of amusement, or fantasy—'I agree, Monsieur!

on a condition.   To prove your penitence, you
shall bring it to me yourself.'.

I professed that her favour overpowered me.
She named an hour when she would be at
home : an address in the Avenue des Champs
Elysées, which I noted on my tablets.

'Not adieu, then Monsieur !   but *au revoir.*'

I bowed perplexedly, holding the curtain aside
to let her sweep through ; and once more she
turned back, gathering up her voluminous train,
to repeat with a glance and accent, which I found
mystifying : 'Remember, Monsieur !   It is only
au revoir.'

That last glimpse of her, with the strange
mockery and an almost elfish malice in her fine
eyes, went home with me later to cause vague
disquiet and fresh suspicion of her truth.   The
spell of her extraordinary, personal charm removed, doubt would assert itself.   Was she quite
sincere ?   Was her fascination not a questionable
one ?   Might not that almost childish outburst
of a grief so touching, and at the time convincing,
be after all factitious; the movement of a born
actress and enchauntress of men, quick to seize
as by a nice professional instinct the opportunity
of an effect ?   Had her whole attitude been a
deliberate pose, a sort of trick ?   The sudden

changes in her subtile voice, the under current of mockery in an invitation which seemed inconsequent, put me on my guard, reinforced all my deep-seated prejudices against the candour of the feminine soul. It left me with a vision of her, fantastically vivid, raccounting to an intimate circle, to an accompaniment of some discreet laughter and the popping of champagne corks, the success of her imposition, the sentimental concessions which she had extorted from a notorious student of cynical moods.

A dangerous woman ! cried Mrs Destrier with the world, which might conceivably be right; at least I was fain to add, a woman whose laughter would be merciless. Certainly, I had no temper for adventures; and a visit to Madame Romanoff on so sentimental an errand seemed to me, the more I pondered it, to partake of this quality to be rich in distasteful possibilities. Must I write myself pusillanimous, if I confess that I never made it, that I committed my old friend's violin into the hands of the woman who had been his pupil by the vulgar aid of a *commissionaire* ?

Pusillanimous or simply prudent; or perhaps cruelly unjust, to a person who had paid penalties and greatly needed kindness ? It is a point I have never been able to decide, though I have tried to raise theories on the ground of her acquiescence. It seemed to me on the cards, that my fiddle bestowed so cavalierly, should be refused. And yet even the fact of her retaining it is open to two interpretations, and Cristich testified for her. Maurice Cristich! Madame Romanoff! the renowned Romanoff, Maurice Cristich! Have I been pusillanimous, prudent or merely cruel? For the life of me I cannot say!

SOUVENIRS OF AN EGOIST

SOUVENIRS OF AN EGOIST

EHEU FUGACES! How that air carries me back, that air ground away so unmercifully, *sans* tune, *sans* time on a hopelessly discordant barrel-organ, right underneath my window. It is being bitterly execrated, I know, by the literary gentleman who lives in chambers above me, and by the convivial gentleman who has a dinner party underneath. It has certainly made it impossible for me to continue the passage in my new Fugue in A minor, which was being transferred so flowingly from my own brain on to the score when it interrupted me. But for all that, I have a shrewd suspicion that I shall bear its unmusical torture as long as it lasts, and eventually send away the frowsy foreigner, who no doubt is playing it, happy with a fairly large coin.

Yes: for the sake of old times, for the old

emotion's sake—for Ninette's sake, I put up with
it, not altogether sorry for the recollections it
has aroused.

How vividly it brings it all back ! Though I
am a rich man now, and so comfortably domi-
ciled; though the fashionable world are so eager
to lionise me, and the musical world look upon
me almost as a god, and to-morrow hundreds of
people will be turned away, for want of space,
from the Hall where I am to play, just I alone,
my last Fantaisie, it was not so very many years
ago that I trudged along, fiddling for half-pence
in the streets. Ninette and I—Ninette with
her barrel-organ, and I fiddling. Poor little
Ninette—that air was one of the four her organ
played. I wonder what has become of her ?
Dead, I should hope, poor child. Now that I am
successful and famous, a Baron of the French
Empire, it is not altogether unpleasant to think
of the old, penniless, vagrant days, by a blazing
fire in a thick carpeted room, with the November
night shut outside. I am rather an epicure of
my emotions, and my work is none the worse
for it.

'Little egoist,' I remember Lady Greville once
said of me, ' he has the true artistic susceptibility.
All his sensations are so much grist for his art.

But it is of Ninette, not Lady Greville, that I think to-night, Ninette's childish face that the dreary grinding organ brings up before me, not Lady Greville's aquiline nose and delicate artificial complexion.

Although I am such a great man now, I should find it very awkward to be obliged to answer questions as to my parentage and infancy. Even my nationality I could not state precisely, though I know I am as much Italian as English, perhaps rather more. From Italy I have inherited my genius and enthusiasm for art, from England I think I must have got my common-sense, and the capacity of keeping the money which I make ; also a certain natural coldness of disposition, which those who only know me as a public character do not dream of. All my earliest memories are very vague and indistinct. I remember tramping over France and Italy with a man and woman—they were Italian, I believe—who beat me, and a fiddle, which I loved passionately, and which I cannot remember having ever been without. They are very shadowy presences now, and the name of the man I have forgotten. The woman, I think, was called Maddalena. I am ignorant whether they were related to me in any way ;

I know that I hated them bitterly, and eventually, after a worse beating than usual, ran away from them. I never cared for any one except my fiddle, until I knew Ninette.

I was very hungry and miserable indeed when that rencontre came about. I wonder sometimes what would have happened if Ninette had not come to the rescue, just at that particular juncture. Would some other salvation have appeared, or would—well, well, if one once begins wondering what would have happened if certain accidents in one's life had not befallen one when they did, where will one come to a stop? Anyhow, when I had escaped from my taskmasters, a wretched, puny child of ten, undersized and shivering, clasping a cheap fiddle in my arms, lost in the huge labyrinth of Paris, without a *sou* in my rags to save me from starvation, I *did* meet Ninette, and that, after all, is the main point.

It was at the close of my first day of independence, a wretched November evening, very much like this one. I had wandered about all day, but my efforts had not been rewarded by a single coin. My fiddle was old and warped, and injured by the rain; its whining was even more repugnant to my own sensitive ear, than to that of the casual passer-by. I was in despair. How I hated all

the few well-dressed, well-to-do people who were
but on the Boulevards, on that inclement night.
I wandered up and down hoping against hope,
until I was too tired to stand, and then I crawled
under the shelter of a covered passage, and flung
myself down on the ground, to die, as I hoped,
crying bitterly.

The alley was dark and narrow, and I did not
see at first that it had another occupant. Presently a hand was put out and touched me on
the shoulder.

I started up in terror, though the touch was
soft and need not have alarmed me. I found it
came from a little girl, for she was really about
my own age, though then she seemed to me
very big and protecting. But she was tall and
strong for her age, and I, as I have said, was
weak and undersized.

'Chut! little boy,' said Ninette ; 'what are
you crying for ?'

And I told her my story, as clearly as I could,
through my sobs ; and soon a pair of small arms
·were thrown round my neck, and a smooth little
face laid against my wet one caressingly. I felt
as if half my troubles were over.

'Don't cry, little boy' said Ninette grandly ;
'I will take care of you. If you like, you shall

live with me. We will make a *ménage* together. What is your profession ? '

I showed her my fiddle, and the sight of its
condition caused fresh tears to flow.

' Ah ! ' she said, with a smile of approval, 'a
violinist—good ! I too am an artiste. You ask
my instrument ? There it is ! '

And she pointed to an object on the ground
beside her, which I had, at first, taken to be a
big box, and dimly hoped might contain eatables.
My respect for my new friend suffered a little
diminution. Already I felt instinctively that to
play the fiddle, even though it is an old, a poor
one, is to be something above a mere organ-
grinder.

But I did not express this feeling—was not
this little girl going to take me home with her ?
would not she, doubtless, give me something to
eat ?

My first impulse was an artistic one ; that
was of Italy. The concealment of it was due
to the English side of me—the practical side.

I crept close to the little girl ; she drew me to
her protectingly.

' What is thy name, *p'tit* ? ' she said.

' Anton,' I answered, for that was what the
woman Maddalena had called me. Her husband,

if he was her husband, never gave me any title, except when he was abusing me, and then my names were many and unmentionable. Nowadays I am the Baron Antonio Antonelli, of the Legion of Honour, but that is merely an extension of the old concise Anton, 'so far as I know, the only name I ever had.'

' Anton ? ' repeated the little girl, that is a nice name to say.   Mine is Ninette.'

We sat in silence in our sheltered nook, waiting until the rain should stop, and very soon I began to whimper again.

'I am so hungry, Ninette,' I said ; 'I have eaten nothing to-day.'

In the literal sense this was a lie ; I had eaten some stale crusts in the early morning, before I gave my taskmasters the slip, but the hunger was true enough.

Ninette began to reproach herself for not thinking of this before. After much fumbling in her pocket, she produced a bit of *brioche*, an apple, and some cold chestnuts.

' *V'la*, Anton,' she said ' pop those in your mouth.   When we get home we will have supper together.   I have bread and milk at home.   And we will buy two hot potatoes from the man on the *quai*.'

I ate the unsatisfying morsels ravenously, Ninette watching me with an approving nod the while. When they were finished, the weather was a little better, and Ninette said we might move. She slung the organ over her shoulder —it was a small organ, though heavy for a child; but she was used to it, and trudged along under its weight like a woman. With her free hand she caught hold of me and led me along the wet streets, proudly home. Ninette's home! Poor little Ninette! It was colder and barer than these rooms of mine now; it had no grand piano, and no thick carpets; and in the place of pictures and *bibelots*, its walls were only wreathed in cobwebs. Still it was drier than the streets of Paris, and if it had been a palace it could not have been more welcome to me than it was that night.

The *ménage* of Ninette was a strange one! There was a tumbledown deserted house in the Montparnasse district. It stood apart, in an overgrown weedy garden, and has long ago been pulled down. It was uninhabited; no one but a Parisian *gamine* could have lived in it, and Ninette had long occupied it, unmolested, save by the rats. Through the broken palings in the garden she had no difficulty in passing, and as its back door had fallen to pieces, there was

nothing to bar her further entry. In one of
the few rooms which had its window intact,
right at the top of the house, a mere attic,
Ninette had installed herself and her scanty
goods, and henceforward this became my home
also.

It has struck me since as strange that the
child's presence should not have been resented
by the owner. But I fancy the house had some
story connected with it. It was, I believe, the
property of an old and infirm miser, who in his re-
luctance to part with any of his money in repairs
had overreached himself, and let his property
become valueless. He could not let it, and he
would not pull it down. It remained therefore
an eyesore to the neighbourhood, until his death
put it in the possession of a less avaricious suc-
cessor. The proprietor never came near the
place, and with the neighbours it had a bad
repute, and they avoided it as much as possible.
It stood, as I have said, alone, and in its own
garden, and Ninette's occupation of it may have
passed unnoticed, while even if any one of the
poor people living around had known of her, it
was, after all, nobody's business to interfere.

When I was last in Paris I went to look for
the house, but all traces of it had vanished, and

G

over the site, so far as I could fix it, a narrow
street of poor houses flourished.

Ninette introduced me to her domain with a
proud air of ownership. She had a little store
of charcoal, with which she proceeded to light a
fire in the grate, and by its fitful light prepared
our common supper—-bread and radishes, washed
down by a pennyworth of milk, of which, I have
no doubt, I received the lion's share. As a
dessert we munched, with much relish, the
steaming potatoes that Ninette had bought from
a stall in the street, and had kept warm in the
pocket of her apron.

And so, as Ninette said, we made a *ménage*
together. How that old organ brings it all back.
My fiddle was useless after the hard usage it
received that day. Ninette and I went out on
our rounds together, but for the present I was a
sleeping partner in the firm, and all I could do
was to grind occasionally when Ninette's arm
ached, or pick up the sous that were thrown us.
Ninette was, as a rule, fairly successful. Since
her mother had died, a year before, leaving her
the organ as her sole legacy, she had lived
mainly by that instrument ; although she often
increased her income in the evenings, when
organ-grinding was more than ever at a discount,

by selling bunches of violets and other flowers as button-holes.

With her organ she had a regular beat, and a distinct *clientèle*. Children playing with their *bonnes* in the gardens of the Tuileries and the Luxembourg were her most productive patrons. Of course we had bad days as well as good, and in winter it was especially bad; but as a rule we managed fairly to make both ends meet. Sometimes we carried home as much as five francs as the result of the day's campaign, but this, of course, was unusual.

Ninette was not precisely a pretty child, but she had a very bright face, and wonderful gray eyes. When she smiled, which was often, her face was very attractive, and a good many people were induced to throw a sou for the smile which they would have assuredly grudged to the music.

Though we were about the same age, the position which it might have been expected we should occupy was reversed. It was Ninette who petted and protected me—I who clung to her.

I was very fond of Ninette, certainly. I should have died in those days if it had not been for her, and sometimes I am surprised at the tenacity of my tenderness for her. As much as I ever cared for anything except my art, I cared for Ninette. But still she was never the first with me, as I must have been with her. I was often fretful and discontented, sometimes, I fear, ready to reproach her for not taking more pains to alleviate our misery, but all the time of our partnership Ninette never gave me a cross word. There was something maternal about her affection, which withstood all ungratefulness. She was always ready to console me when I was miserable, and throw her arms round me and kiss me when I was cold; and many a time, I am sure, when the day's earnings had been scanty, the little girl must have gone to sleep hungry, that I might not be stinted in my supper.

One of my grievances, and that the sorest of all, · was the loss of my beloved fiddle. This, for all her goodwill, Ninette was powerless to allay.

' Dear Anton,' she said, ' do not mind about it. I earn enough for both with my organ, and some day we shall save enough to buy thee a new fiddle. When we are together, and have got food and charcoal, what does it matter about an old fiddle ? Come, eat thy supper, Anton, and I will light the fire. Never mind, dear Anton.'

And she laid her soft little cheek against mine
with a pleading look.

' Don't,' I cried, pushing her away, 'you can't
understand, Ninette; you can only grind an organ
—just four tunes, always the same.   But I loved
my fiddle, loved it! loved it!' I cried passionately.   'It could talk to me, Ninette, and tell
me beautiful, new things, always beautiful, and
always new.   Oh, Ninette, I shall die if I cannot
play!'

It was always the same cry, and Ninette, if she
could not understand, and was secretly a little
jealous, was as distressed as I was; but what
could she do?

Eventually, I got my violin, and it was Ninette
who gave it me.   The manner of its acquirement
was in this wise.

Ninette would sometimes invest some of her
savings in violets, which she divided with me, and
made into nosegays for us to sell in the streets at
night.

Theatre doors and frequented places on the
Boulevards were our favourite spots.

One night we had taken up our station outside
the Opéra, when a gentleman stopped on his way
in, and asked Ninette for a button-hole.   He
was in evening dress and in a great hurry.

'How much?' he asked shortly.

'Ten *sous*, *M'sieu*,' said exorbitant little Ninette, expecting to get two at the most.

The gentleman drew out some coins hastily and selected a bunch from the basket.

'Here is a franc,' he said, 'I cannot wait for change,' and putting a coin into Ninette's hand he turned into the theatre.

Ninette ran towards me with her eyes gleaming; she held up the piece of money exultantly.

'Tiens, Anton!' she cried, and I saw that it was not a franc, as we had thought at first, but a gold Napoleon.

I believe the good little boy and girl in the story-books would have immediately sought out the unfortunate gentleman and bid him rectify his mistake, generally receiving, so the legend runs, a far larger bonus as a reward of their integrity. I have never been a particularly good little boy, however, and I don't think it ever struck either Ninette or myself—perhaps we were not sufficiently speculative—that any other course was open to us than to profit by the mistake. Ninette began to consider how we were to spend it.'

'Think of it, Anton, a whole gold *louis*. A *louis*,' said Ninette, counting laboriously, 'is

twenty francs, a franc is twenty sous, Anton;
how many sous are there in a louis? More than
an hundred?'

But this piece of arithmetic was beyond me;
I shook my head dubiously.

'What shall we buy first, Anton?' said Ninette,
with sparkling eyes. 'You shall have new
things, Anton, a pair of new shoes and an hat;
and I—'

But I had other things than clothes in my
mind's eye; I interrupted her.

'Ninette, dear little Ninette,' I said coaxingly,
'remember the fiddle.'

Ninette's face fell, but she was a tender little
thing, and she showed no hesitation.

'Certainly, Anton,' she said, but with less
enthusiasm, 'we will get it to-morrow — one
of the fiddles you showed me in M. Boudinot's
shop on the Quai. Do you think the ten-franc
one will do, or the light one for fifteen
francs?'

'Oh, the light one, dear Ninette,' I said; 'it
is worth more than the extra money. Besides,
we shall soon earn it back now. Why if you
could earn such a lot as you have with your old
organ, when you only have to turn an handle,
think what a lot I shall make, fiddling. For

you have to be something to play the fiddle, Ninette.'

'Yes,' said the little girl, wincing; 'you are right, dear Anton. Perhaps you will get rich and go away and leave me?'

'No, Ninette,' I declared grandly, 'I will always take care of you. I have no doubt I shall get rich, because I am going to be a great musician, but I shall not leave you. I will have a big house on the Champs Elysées, and then you shall come and live with me, and be my housekeeper. And in the evenings, I will play to you and make you open your eyes, Ninette. You will like me to play, you know; we are often dull in the evenings.'

'Yes,' said Ninette meekly, 'we will buy your fiddle to-morrow, dear Anton. Let us go home now.'

Poor vanished Ninette! I must often have made the little heart sore with some of the careless things I said. Yet looking back at it now, I know that I never cared for any living person so much as I did for Ninette.

I have very few illusions left now ; a childhood, such as mine, does not tend to preserve them, and time and success have not made me less cynical. Still I have never let my scepticism touch that childish presence. Lady Greville once said to me, in the presence of her nephew Felix Leominster, a musician too, like myself, that we three were curiously suited, for that we were, without exception, the three most cynical persons in the universe. Perhaps in a way she was right. Yet for all her cynicism Lady Greville I know has a bundle of old and faded letters, tied up in black ribbon in some hidden drawer, that perhaps she never reads now, but that she cannot forget or destroy. They are in a bold handwriting, that is, not, I think, that of the miserable, old debauchee, her husband, from whom she has been separated since the first year of her marriage, and their envelopes bear Indian postmarks.

And Felix, who told me the history of those letters with a smile of pity on his thin, ironical lips—Felix, whose principles are adapted to his conscience and whose conscience is bounded by the law, and in whom I believe as little as he does in me, I found out by accident not so very long ago. It was on the day of All Souls, the melancholy festival of souvenirs, celebrated once a year, under the November fogs, that I strayed into the Montparnasse Cemetery, to seek inspiration for my art. And though he did not see me, I saw Felix, the prince of railers, who believes in nothing and cares for nothing except himself, for music is not with him a passion but an *agrément*. Felix bareheaded, and without his usual smile, putting fresh flowers on the grave of a little Parisian grisette, who had been his mistress and died five years ago. I thought of Balzac's 'Messe de l' Athée' and ranked Felix's inconsistency with it, feeling at the same time how natural such a paradox is. And myself, the last of the trio, at the mercy of a street organ, I cannot forget Ninette.

Though it was not until many years had passed that I heard that little criticism, the purchase of my fiddle was destined very shortly to bring my life in contact with its author. Those were the days when a certain restraint grew up between Ninette and myself. Ninette, it must be confessed, was jealous of the fiddle. Perhaps she knew instinctively that music was with me a single and absorbing passion, from which she was excluded. She was no genius, little Ninette, and her organ was nothing more to her than the means of making a livelihood; she felt not the smallest *tendresse* for it, and could not understand why a dead and inanimate fiddle, made of mere

wood and catgut, should be any more to me than
that.   How could she know that to me it was
never a dead thing, that even when it hung hopelessly out of my reach, in the window of M.
Boudinot, before ever it had given out wild,
impassioned music beneath my hands, it was
always a live thing to me, alive and with a
human, throbbing heart, vibrating with hope and
passion.

So Ninette was jealous of the fiddle, and being
proud in her way, she became more and more
quiet and reticent, and drew herself aloof from
me, although, wrapped up as I was in the double
egoism of art and boyhood, I failed to notice
this.   I have been sorry since that any shadow
of misunderstanding should have clouded the
closing days of our partnership.   It is late to
regret now, however.   When my fiddle was
added to our belongings, we took to going out
separately.   It was more profitable, and, besides,
Ninette, I think, saw that I was growing a little
ashamed of her organ.   On one of these occasions,
as I played before a house in the Faubourg St
Germain, the turning point of my life befell me.
The house, outside which I had taken my station
was a large, white one, with a balcony on the
first floor.   This balcony was unoccupied, but

the window looking to it was open, and through
the lace curtains I could distinguish the sound
of vioces.   I began to play; at first, one of the
airs that Maddalena had taught me ; but before
it was finished, I had glided off, as usual, into
an improvisation.

When I was playing like that, I threw all my
soul into my fingers, and I had neither ears nor
eyes for anything around me.   I did not therefore notice until I had finished playing that a
lady and a young man had come out into the
balcony, and were beckoning to me.

'Bravo!' cried the lady enthusiastically, but
she did not throw me the reward I had expected.
She turned and said something to her companion,
who smiled and disappeared.   I waited ex-
pectantly, thinking perhaps she had sent him for
her purse.   Presently the door opened, and the
young man issued from it.   He came to me and
touched me on the shoulder.

'You are to come with me,' he said, authorita-
tively, speaking in French, but with an English
accent.   I followed him, my heart beating with
excitement, through the big door, into a large,
handsome hall and up a broad staircase, thinking
that in all my life I had never seen such a
beautiful house.

He led me into a large and luxurious *salon*, which seemed to my astonished eyes like a wonderful museum. The walls were crowded with pictures, a charming composition by Gustave Moreau was lying on the grand piano, waiting until a nook could be found for it to hang. Renaissance bronzes and the work of eighteenth century silversmiths jostled one another on brackets, and on a table lay a handsome violin-case. The pale blinds were drawn down, and there was a delicious smell of flowers diffused everywhere. A lady was lying on a sofa near the window, a handsome woman of about thirty, whose dress was a miracle of lace and flimsiness.

The young man led me towards her, and she placed two delicate, jewelled hands on my shoulders, looking me steadily in the face.

'Where did you learn to play like that, my boy?' she asked.

'I cannot remember when I could not fiddle, Madame,' I answered, and that was true.

'The boy is a born musician, Felix,' said Lady Greville. 'Look at his hands.'

And she held up mine to the young man's notice; he glanced at them carelessly.

'Yes, Miladi,' said the young man, 'they are

real violin hands.   What were you playing just
now, my lad ? '

'I don't know, sir,' I said.   'I play just what
comes into my head.'

Lady Greville looked at her nephew with a
glance of triumph.

'What did I tell you ? ' she cried.   'The boy
is a genius, Felix.   I shall have him educated.'

'All your geese are swans, Auntie,' said the
young man in English.

Lady Greville, however, ignored this thrust

'Will you play for me now, my dear,' she said
'as you did before—just what comes into your
head ? '

I nodded, and was getting my fiddle to my
chin, when she stopped me.

'Not that thing,' bestowing a glance of
contempt at my instrument.   'Felix, the
Stradivarius.'

The young man went to the other side of the
room, and returned with the case which I had
noticed.   He put it in my hand, with the
injunction to handle it gently.   I had never
heard of Cremona violins, nor of my namesake
Stradivarius; but at the sight of the dark
seasoned wood, reposing on its blue velvet, I
could not restrain a cry of admiration.

I have that same instrument in my room now, and I would not trust it in the hands of another for a million.

I lifted the violin tenderly from its case, and ran my bow up the gamut.

I felt almost intoxicated at the mellow sounds it uttered. I could have kissed the dark wood, that looked to me stained through and through with melody.

I began to play. My improvisation was a song of triumph and delight; the music, at first rapid and joyous, became slower and more solemn, as the inspiration seized on me, until at last, in spite of myself, it grew into a wild and indescribable dirge, fading away in a long wail of unutterable sadness and regret. When it was over I felt exhausted and unstrung, as though virtue had gone out from me. I had played as I had never played before. The young man had turned away, and was looking out of the window. The lady on the sofa was transfigured. The languor had altogether left her, and the tears were streaming down her face, to the great detriment of the powder and enamel which composed her complexion.

She pulled me towards her, and kissed me.

'It is beautiful, terrible!' she said; 'I have

never heard such strange music in my life. You must stay with me now and have masters. If you can play like that now, without culture and education, in time, when you have been taught, you will be the greatest violinist that ever lived.'

I will say of Lady Greville that, in spite of her frivolity and affectations, she does love music at the bottom of her soul, with the absorbing passion that in my eyes would absolve a person for committing all the sins in the Decalogue. If her heart could be taken out and examined I can fancy it as a shield, divided into equal fields. Perhaps, as her friends declare, one of these might bear the device 'Modes et Confections'; but I am sure that you would see on the other, even more deeply graven, the divine word 'Music.'

She is one of the few persons whose praise of any of my compositions gives me real satisfaction; and almost alone, when everybody is running, in true goose fashion, to hear my piano recitals, she knows and tells me to stick to my true vocation—the violin.

'My dear Baron,' she said, 'why waste your time playing on an instrument which is not suited to you, when you have Stradivarius waiting at home for the magic touch?'

She was right, though it is the fashion to speak of me now as a second Rubenstein. There are two or three finer pianists than I, even here in England. But I am quite sure, yes, and you are sure, too, oh my Stradivarius, that in the whole world there is nobody who can make such music out of you as I can, no one to whom you tell such stories as you tell to me. Anyone, who knows, could see by merely looking at my hands that they are violin and not piano hands.

'Will you come and live with me, Anton?' said Lady Greville, more calmly. 'I am rich, and childless; you shall live just as if you were my child. The best masters in Europe shall teach you. Tell me where to find your parents, Anton, and I will see them to-night.'

'I have no parents,' I said, 'only Ninette. I cannot leave Ninette.'

'Shade of Musset, who is Ninette?' asked Felix, turning round from the window.

I told him.

'What is to be done?' cried Lady Greville in perplexity. 'I cannot have the girl here as well, and I will not let my Phœnix go.'

'Send her to the Sœurs de la Miséricorde,' said the young man carelessly; 'you have a nomination.'

H

'Have I?' said Lady Greville, with a laugh. 'I am sure I did not know it. It is an excellent idea; but do you think he will come without the other? I suppose they were like brother and sister?'

'Look at him now,' said Felix, pointing to where I stood caressing the precious wood; 'he would sell his soul for that fiddle.'

Lady Greville took the hint. 'Here, Anton,' said she, 'I cannot have Ninette here—you understand, once and for all. But I will see that she is sent to a kind home, where she will want for nothing and be trained up as a servant. You need not bother about her. You will live with me and be taught, and some day, if you are good and behave, you shall go and see Ninette.'

I was irresolute, but I only said doggedly, feeling what would be the end, 'I do not want to come, if Ninette may not.'

Then Lady Greville played her trump card.

'Look, Anton,' she said, 'you see that violin. I have no need, I see, to tell you its value. If you will come with me and make no scene, you shall have it for your very own. Ninette will be perfectly happy. Do you agree?'

I looked at my old fiddle, lying on the floor.

How yellow and trashy it looked beside the grand old Cremona, bedded in its blue velvet.

'I will do what you like, Madame,' I said.

'Human nature is pretty much the same in geniuses and dullards,' said Felix. 'I congratulate you, Auntie.'

And so the bargain was struck, and the new life entered upon that very day. Lady Greville sought out Ninette at once, though I was not allowed to accompany her.

I never saw Ninette again. She made no opposition to Lady Greville's scheme. She let herself be taken to the Orphanage, and she never asked, so they said, to see me again.

'She's a stupid little thing,' said Lady Greville to her nephew, on her return, 'and as plain as possible ; but I suppose she was kind to the boy. They will forget each other now I hope. It is not as if they were related.'

'In that case they would already be hating each other. However, I am quite sure your protégé will forget soon enough ; and, after all, you have nothing to do with the girl.'

I suppose I did not think very much of Ninette then ; but what would you have ? It was such a change from the old vagrant days, that there is a good deal to excuse me. I was absorbed too

in the new and wonderful symmetry which music
began to assume, as taught me by the master
Lady Greville procured for me.   When the
news was broken to me, with great gentleness,
that my little companion had run away from the
sisters with whom she had been placed—run
away, and left no traces behind her, I hardly
realised how completely she would have passed
away from me.   I thought of her for a little while
with some regret ; then I remembered Stradivarius, and I could not be sorry long.   So by
degrees I ceased to think of her.

I lived on in Lady Greville's house, going with
her, wherever she stayed—London, Paris, and
Nice—until I was thirteen.   Then she sent me
away to study music at a small German capital,
in the house of one of the few surviving pupils
of Weber.   We parted as we had lived together,
without affection.

Personally Lady Greville did not like me ; if
anything, she felt an actual repugnance towards
me.   All the care she lavished on me was for the
sake of my talent, not for myself.   She took a
great deal of trouble in superintending, not only
my musical education, but my general culture.
She designed little mediæval costumes for me,
and was indefatigable in her endeavours to im-

part to my manners that finish which a gutter education had denied me.

There is a charming portrait of me, by a well-known English artist, that hangs now in her ladyship's drawing-room. A pale boy of twelve, clad in an old-fashioned suit of ruby velvet ; a boy with huge, black eyes, and long curls of the same colour, is standing by an oak music-stand, holding before him a Cremona violin, whose rich colouring is relieved admirably by the beautiful old point lace with which the boy's doublet is slashed. It is a charming picture. The famous artist who painted it considers it his best portrait, and Lady Greville is proud of it.

But her pride is of the same quality as that which made her value my presence. I was in her eyes merely the complement of her famous fiddle.

I heard her one day express a certain feeling of relief at my approaching departure.

'You regret having taken him up?' asked her nephew curiously.

'No,' she said, 'that would be folly. He repays all one's trouble, as soon as he touches his fiddle—but I don't like him.'

'He can play like the great Pan,' says Felix.

'Yes, and like Pan he is half a beast.'

'You may make a musician out of him,' answered the young man, examining his pink nails with a certain admiration, 'but you will never make him a gentleman.'

'Perhaps not,' said Lady Greville carelessly. 'Still, Felix, he is very refined.'

Dame! I think he would own himself mistaken now. Mr Felix Leominster himself is not a greater social success than the Baron Antonio Antonelli, of the Legion of Honour. I am as sensitive as anyone to the smallest spot on my linen, and Duchesses rave about my charming manners.

For the rest my souvenirs are not very numerous. I lived in Germany until I made my *début*, and I never heard anything more of Ninette.

The history of my life is very much the history of my art : and that you know. I have always been an art-concentrated man—self-concentrated, my friend Felix Leominster tells me frankly— and since I was a boy nothing has ever troubled the serene repose of my egoism.

It is strange considering the way people rant about the 'passionate sympathy' of my playing, the 'enormous potentiality of suffering' revealed in my music, how singularly free from passion and disturbance my life has been.

I have never let myself be troubled by what is commonly called 'love.' To be frank with you, I do not much believe in it. Of the two principal elements of which it is composed, vanity and egoism, I have too little of the former, too much of the latter, too much coldness withal in my character to suffer from it. My life has been notoriously irreproachable. I figure in polemical literature as an instance of a man who has lived in contact with the demoralising influence of the stage, and will yet go to Heaven. *A la bonne heure !*

I am coming to the end of my souvenirs and of my cigar at the same time. I must convey a coin somehow to that dreary person outside, who is grinding now half-way down the street.

On consideration, I decide emphatically against opening the window and presenting it that way. If the fog once gets in, it will utterly spoil me for any work this evening. I feel myself in travail also of two charming little *Lieder* that all this thinking about Ninette has suggested. How would 'Chansons de Gamine' do for a title ? I think it best, on second thoughts, to ring for Giacomo, my man, and send him out with the half-crown I propose to sacrifice on the altar of sentiment. Doubtless the musician is a country-woman of his, and if he pockets the coin, that is his look out.

Now if I was writing a romance, what a chance I have got. I should tell you how my organ-grinder turned out to be no other than Ninette. Of course she would not be spoilt or changed by the years—just the same Ninette. Then what scope for a pathetic scene of reconciliation and forgiveness—the whole to conclude with a peal of marriage bells, two people living together 'happy ever after.' But I am not writing a romance, and I am a musician, not a poet.

Sometimes, however, it strikes me that I should like to see Ninette again, and I find myself seeking traces of her in childish faces in the street.

The absurdity of such an expectation strikes me very forcibly afterwards, when I look at my reflection in the glass, and tell myself that I must be careful in the disposition of my parting.

Ninette, too, was my contemporary. Still I cannot conceive of her as a woman. To me she is always a child. Ninette grown up, with a draggled dress and squalling babies, is an incongruous thing that shocks my sense of artistic fitness. My fiddle is my only mistress, and while I can summon its consolation at command, I may not be troubled by the pettiness of a merely human love. But once when I was down with Roman fever, and tossed on a hotel bed, all the long, hot night, while Giacomo drowsed in a corner over 'Il Diavolo Rosa,' I seemed to miss Ninette.

Remembering that time, I sometimes fancy that when the inevitable hour strikes, and this hand is too weak to raise the soul of melody out of Stradivarius—when, my brief dream of life and music over, I go down into the dark land, where there is no more music, and no Ninette, into the sleep from which there comes no awaking, I should like to see her again, not the woman but the child. I should like to look into the wonderful eyes of the old Ninette, to feel the soft cheek laid against mine, to hold the little brown hands, as in the old *gamin* days.

It is a foolish thought, because I am not forty yet, and with the moderate life I lead I may live to play Stradivarius for another thirty years.

There is always the hope, too, that it, when it comes, may seize me suddenly. To see it coming, that is the horrible part. I should like to be struck by lightning, with you in my arms, Stradivarius, oh, my beloved—to die playing.

The literary gentleman over my head is stamping viciously about his room. What would his language be if he knew how I have rewarded his tormentress—he whose principles are so strict that he would bear the agony for hours, sooner than give a barrel-organ sixpence to go to another street. He would be capable of giving Giacomo a sovereign to pocket my coin, if he only knew. Yet I owe that unmusical old organ a charming evening, tinged with the faint *soupçon* of melancholy which is necessary to and enhances the highest pleasure. Over the memories it has excited I have smoked a pleasant cigar—peace to its ashes!

THE STATUTE OF LIMITATIONS

DURING five years of an almost daily association with Michael Garth, in a solitude of Chili, which threw us, men of common speech, though scarcely of common interests, largely on each other's tolerance, I had grown, if not into an intimacy with him, at least into a certain familiarity, through which the salient features of his history, his character reached me. It was a singular character, and an history rich in instruction. So much I gathered from hints, which he let drop long before I had heard the end of it. Unsympathetic as the man was to me, it was impossible not to be interested by it. As our acquaintance advanced, it took (his character I mean) more and more the aspect of a difficult problem in psychology, that I was passionately interested in solving: to study it was my recreation, after watching the fluctuating course of nitrates. So that when I had achieved fortune, and might have started home immediately, my interest induced me to wait more than three months, and return in the same ship with him. It was through this delay that I am enabled to transcribe the issue of my impressions : I found them edifying, if only for their singular irony.

From his own mouth indeed I gleaned but little ; although during our voyage home, in those long nights when we paced the deck together under the Southern Cross, his reticence occasionally gave way, and I obtained glimpses of a more intimate knowledge of him than the whole of our juxtaposition on the station had ever afforded me. I guessed more, however, than he told me ; and what was lacking I pieced together later, from the talk of the girl to whom I broke the news of his death. He named her to me, for the first time, a day or two before that happened : a piece of confidence so unprecedented, that I must have been blind, indeed, not to have foreseen what it prefaced. I had seen her face the first time I entered his house, where her photograph hung on a conspicuous wall : the charming, oval face of a young girl, little more than a child, with great eyes, that one

guessed, one knew not why, to be the colour of
violets, looking out with singular wistfulness
from a waving cloud of dark hair. Afterwards,
he told me that it was the picture of his *fiancée* :
but, before that, signs had not been wanting by
which I had read a woman in his life.

Iquique is not Paris ; it is not even Valparaiso ;
but it is a city of civilization ; and but two days'
ride from the pestilential stew, where we nursed
our lives doggedly on quinine and hope, the
ultimate hope of evasion. The lives of most
Englishmen yonder, who superintend works in
the interior, are held on the same tenure : you
know them by a certain savage, hungry look in
their eyes. In the meantime, while they wait
for their luck, most of them are glad enough
when buisness calls them down for a day or two
to Iquique. There are shops and streets, lit
streets through which blackeyed Senoritas pass
in their lace mantilas ; there are *cafés* too ; and
faro for those who reck of it ; and bull fights,
and newspapers younger than six weeks ; and in
the harbour, taking in their fill of nitrates, many
ships, not to be considered without envy, because
they are coming, within a limit of days to
England. But Iquique had no charm for
Michael Garth, and when one of us must go,

it was usually I, his subordinate, who being delegated, congratulated myself on his indifference. Hard-earned dollars melted at Iquique; and to Garth, life in Chili had long been solely a matter of amassing them. So he stayed on, in the prickly heat of Agnas Blancas, and grimly counted the days, and the money (although his nature, I believe, was fundamentally generous, in his set concentration of purpose, he had grown morbidly avaricious) which should restore him to his beautiful mistress. Morose, reticent, unsociable as he had become, he had still, I discovered by degrees, a leaning towards the humanities, a nice taste, such as could only be the result of much knowledge, in the fine things of literature. His infinitesimal library, a few French novels, an Horace, and some well thumbed volumes of the modern English poets in the familiar edition of Tauchnitz, he put at my disposal, in return for a collection, somewhat similar, although a little larger, of my own. In his rare moments of amiability, he could talk on such matters with *verve* and originality : more usually he preferred to pursue with the bitterest animosity an abstract fetish which he called his 'luck.' He was by temperament an enraged pessimist ; and I could believe, that he seriously attributed to Providence, some quality inconceivably malignant, directed in all things personally against himself. His immense bitterness and his careful avarice, alike, I could explain, and in a measure justify, when I came to understand that he had felt the sharpest stings of poverty, and, moreover, was passionately in love, in love *comme on ne l'est plus.* As to what his previous resources had been, I knew nothing, nor why they had failed him ; but I gathered that the crisis had come, just when his life was complicated by the sudden blossoming of an old friendship into love, in his case, at least, to be complete and final. The girl too was poor ; they were poorer than most poor persons : how could he refuse the post, which, through the good offices of a friend, was just then unexpectedly offered him ? Certainly, it was abroad ; it implied five years' solitude in Equatorial America. Separation and change were to be accounted ; perhaps, disease and death, and certainly his 'luck,' which seemed to include all these. But it also promised, when the term of his exile was up, and there were means of shortening it, a certain competence, and very likely wealth ; escaping those other contingencies, marriage. There seemed no other way. The girl was very

I

young : there was no question of an early
marriage ; there was not even a definite engagement. Garth would take no promise from her :
only for himself, he was her bound lover while
he breathed ; would keep himself free to claim
her, when he came back in five years, or ten, or
twenty, if she had not chosen better. He would
not bind her ; but I can imagine how impressive
his dark, bitter face must have made this renunciation to the little girl with the violet eyes ;
how tenderly she repudiated her freedom. She
went out as a governess, and sat down to wait.
And absence only rivetted faster the chain of
her affection : it set Garth more securely on
the pedestal of her idea ; for in love it is most
usually the reverse of that social maxim, *les
absents ont toujours tort*, which is true.

Garth, on his side, writing to her, month by
month, while her picture smiled on him from
the wall, if he was careful always to insist on her
perfect freedom, added, in effect, so much more
than this, that the renunciation lost its benefit.
He lived in a dream of her ; and the memory
of her eyes and her hair was a perpetual presence
with him, less ghostly than the real company
among whom he mechanically transacted his
daily business. Burnt away and consumed by

desire of her living arms, he was counting the hours which still prevented him from them. Yet, when his five years were done, he delayed his return, although his economies had justified it ; settled down for another term of five years, which was to be prolonged to seven. Actually, the memory of his old poverty, with its attendant dishonours, was grown a fury, pursuing him ceaselessly with whips. The lust of gain, always for the girl's sake, and so, as it were, sanctified, had become a second nature to him ; an intimate madness, which left him no peace. His worst nightmare was to wake with a sudden shock, imagining that he had lost everything, that he was reduced to his former poverty : a cold sweat would break all over him before he had mastered the horror. The recurrence of it, time after time, made him vow grimly, that he would go home a rich man, rich enough to laugh at the fantasies of his luck. Latterly, indeed, this seemed to have changed ; so that his vow was fortunately kept. He made money lavishly at last : all his operations were successful, even those which seemed the wildest gambling : and the most forlorn speculations turned round, and shewed a pretty harvest, when Garth meddled with their stock.

And all the time he was waiting there, and scheming, at Agnas Blancas, in a feverish concentration of himself upon his ultimate reunion with the girl at home, the man was growing old: gradually at first, and insensibly ; but towards the end, by leaps and starts, with an increasing consciousness of how he aged and altered, which did but feed his black melancholy. It was borne upon him, perhaps, a little brutally, and not by direct self-examination, when there came another photograph from England. A beautiful face still but certainly the face of a woman, who had passed from the grace of girlhood (seven years now separated her from it), to a dignity touched with sadness : a face, upon which life had already written some of its cruelties. For many days after this arrival, Garth was silent and moody, even beyond his wont : then he studiously concealed it. He threw himself again furiously into his economic battle; he had gone back to the inspiration of that other, older portrait : the charming, oval face of a young girl, almost a child, with great eyes, that one guessed, one knew not why, to be the colour of violets.

As the time of our departure approached, a week or two before we had gone down to Valparaiso, where Garth had business to wind up, I was enabled to study more intimately the morbid demon which possessed him. It was the most singular thing in the world : no man had hated the country more, had been more passionately determined for a period of years to escape from it; and now that his chance was come the emotion with which he viewed it was nearer akin to terror than to the joy of a reasonable man who is about to compass the desire of his life. He had kept the covenant which he had made with himself; he was a rich man, richer than he had ever meant to be. Even now he was full of vigour, and not much past the threshold of middle age, and he was going home to the woman whom for the best part of fifteen years he had adored with an unexampled constancy, whose fidelity had been to him all through that exile as the shadow of a rock in a desert land : he was going home to an honourable marriage. But withal he was a man with an incurable sadness ; miserable and afraid. It seemed to me at times that he would have been glad if she had kept her troth less well, had only availed herself of that freedom which he gave her, to disregard her promise. And this was the more strange in that I never doubted the strength of his attachment ; it remained engrossing and un-

changed, the largest part of his life.   No alien
shadow had ever come between him and the
memory of the little girl with the violet eyes, to
whom he at least was bound.   But a shadow
was there ; fantastic it seemed to me at first,
too grotesque to be met with argument, but in
whose very lack of substance, as I came to see,
lay its ultimate strength.   The notion of the
woman, which now she was, came between him
and the girl whom he had loved, whom he still
loved with passion, and separated them.   It was
only on our voyage home, when we walked the
deck together interminably during the hot,
sleepless nights, that he first revealed to me
without subterfuge, the slow agony by which
this phantom slew him.   And his old bitter
conviction of the malignity of his luck, which
had lain dormant in the first flush of his material
prosperity, returned to him.   The apparent
change in it seemed to him just then, the last
irony of those hostile powers which had pursued
him.

    'It came to me suddenly,' he said, 'just before
I left Agnas, when I had been adding up my
pile and saw there was nothing to keep me, that
it was all wrong.   I had been a blamed fool!
I might have gone home years ago.   Where is

the best of my life? Burnt out, wasted, buried
in that cursed oven! Dollars? If I had all the
metal in Chili, I couldn't buy one day of youth.
Her youth too; that has gone with the rest;
that's the worst part!'

Despite all my protests, his despondency increased as the steamer ploughed her way towards
England, with the ceaseless throb of her screw,
which was like the panting of a great beast.
Once, when we had been talking of other matters,
of certain living poets whom he favoured, he
broke off with a quotation from the 'Prince's
Progress' of Miss Rossetti:

> 'Ten years ago, five years ago,
>   One year ago,
> Even then you had arrived in time,
>   Though somewhat slow;
> Then you had known her living face
>   Which now you cannot know.'

He stopped sharply, with a tone in his voice
which seemed to intend, in the lines, a personal
instance.

'I beg your pardon!' I protested. 'I don't
see the analogy. You haven't loitered; you
don't come too late. A brave woman has
waited for you; you have a fine felicity before
you: it should be all the better, because you
have won it laboriously. For Heaven's sake, be

reasonable!' He shook his head sadly; then added, with a gesture of sudden passion, looking out over the taffrail, at the heaving gray waters: 'It's finished. I haven't any longer the courage.' 'Ah!' I exclaimed impatiently, 'say once for all, outright, that you are tired of her, that you want to back out of it.' 'No,' he said drearily, 'it isn't that. I can't reproach myself with the least wavering. I have had a single passion; I have given my life to it; it is there still, consuming me. Only the girl I loved: it's as if she had died. Yes, she is dead, as dead as Helen: and I have not the consolation of knowing where they have laid her. Our marriage will be a ghastly mockery: a marriage of corpses. Her heart, how can she give it me? She gave it years ago to the man I was, the man who is dead. We, who are left, are nothing to one another, mere strangers.'

One could not argue with a perversity so infatuate: it was useless to point out, that in life a distinction so arbitrary as the one which haunted him does not exist. It was only left me to wait, hoping that in the actual event of their meeting, his malady would be healed. But this meeting, would it ever be compassed? There were moments when his dread of it seemed to have grown so extreme, that he would be capable of any cowardice, any compromise to postpone it, to render it impossible. He was afraid that she would read his revulsion in his eyes, would suspect how time and his very constancy had given her the one rival with whom she could never compete ; the memory of her old self, of her gracious girlhood, which was dead. Might not she too, actually, welcome a reprieve ; however readily she would have submitted, out of honour or lassitude, to a marriage which could only be a parody of what might have been ?

At Lisbon, I hoped that he had settled these questions, had grown reasonable and sane, for he wrote a long letter to her which was subsequently a matter of much curiosity to me ; and he wore, for a day or two afterwards, an air almost of assurance which deceived me. I wondered what he had put in that epistle, how far he had explained himself, justified his curious attitude. Or was it simply a *résumé*, a conclusion to those many letters which he had written at Agnas Blancas, the last one which he would ever address to the little girl of the earlier photograph ?

Later, I would have given much to decide

K

this, but she herself, the woman who read it, maintained unbroken silence. In return, I kept a secret from her, my private interpretation of the accident of his death. It seemed to me a knowledge tragical enough for her, that he should have died as he did, so nearly in English waters ; within a few days of the home coming, which they had passionately expected for years.

It would have been mere brutality to afflict her further, by lifting the veil of obscurity, which hangs over that calm, moonless night, by pointing to the note of intention in it. For it is in my experience, that accidents so opportune do not in real life occur, and I could not forget that, from Garth's point of view, death was certainly a solution. Was it not, moreover, precisely a solution, which so little time before he had the appearance of having found? Indeed when the first shock of his death was past, I could feel that it was after all a solution : with his 'luck' to handicap him, he had perhaps avoided worse things than the death he met. For the luck of such a man, is it not his temperament, his character? Can any one escape from that? May it not have been an escape for the poor devil himself, an escape too for the woman who loved him, that he chose to drop down, fathoms

down, into the calm, irrecoverable depths of the
Atlantic, when he did, bearing with him at
least an unspoilt ideal, and leaving her a memory
that experience could never tarnish, nor custom
stale ?

.

.

THE END

List of Books

in

Belles Lettres

ALL THE BOOKS IN THIS CATALOGUE ARE
PUBLISHED AT NET PRICES

London : Elkin Mathews, Vigo Street, W.

1895

Telegraphic Address—
'ELEGANTIA, LONDON.'

List of Books
IN
BELLES LETTRES
(Including some Transfers)

PUBLISHED BY

ELKIN MATHEWS

VIGO STREET, LONDON, W.

N.B.—The Authors and Publisher reserve the right of reprinting any book in this list, except in cases where a stipulation has been made to the contrary, and of printing a separate edition of any of the books for America. In the case of limited Editions, the numbers mentioned do not include the copies sent for review, nor those supplied to the public libraries. The prices of books not yet published are subject to variation.

The Books mentioned in this Catalogue can be obtained to order by any Bookseller. It should be noted also that they are supplied to the Trade on terms which will not allow of discount.

⟞§§⟝

The following are a few of the Authors represented in this Catalogue:

P. ADDLESHAW.	LIONEL JOHNSON.
R. D. BLACKMORE.	CHARLES LAMB.
F. W. BOURDILLON.	RICHARD LE GALLIENNE.
BLISS CARMAN.	P. B. MARSTON.
E. R. CHAPMAN.	HON. RODEN NOEL.
ERNEST DOWSON.	MAY PROBYN.
MICHAEL FIELD.	F. YORK POWELL.
T. GORDON HAKE.	J. A. SYMONDS.
ARTHUR HALLAM.	JOHN TODHUNTER.
KATHARINE HINKSON.	HENRY VAN DYKE.
HERBERT P. HORNE.	THEODORE WATTS.
RICHARD HOVEY.	FREDERICK WEDMORE.
LEIGH HUNT.	P. H. WICKSTEED.
SELWYN IMAGE.	W. B. YEATS.

ABBOTT (DR. C. C.).

TRAVELS IN A TREE-TOP. Sm. 8vo. 5s. *net.*

Philadelphia : J. B. Lippincott Company.

" Dr. Abbott pleases by the interest he takes in the subject which he treats . .
and he adorns his matter with a good English style . . . Altogether, with its
dainty printing, it would be a charming book to read in the open air on a bright
summer's day.—*Athenæum.*

" He has an observant eye, a warm sympathy, and a pen that enables us to see
with him. Nothing could be more restful than to read the thoughts of such nature-
lovers. The very titles of his chapters suggest quiet and gentle things."—*Dublin Herald.*

" A delightful volume this of Nature Sketches. Dr. Abbott writes about New
England woods and streams, scenes neither quite familiar nor quite strange to us who
know the same things in the old country. The severer winter makes some difference,
as, for instance, in the number of birds that migrate there, but are stationary here;
and there are, of course, other differences in both fauna and flora; nevertheless, we
feel, in a way, at home, when Dr. Abbott takes us on one of his delightful winter or
summer excursions. This is a book which we cannot recommend too highly."—
Spectator.

THE BIRDS ABOUT US. 73 Engravings. Second Edition.
Thick cr. 8vo. 5s. 6d. *net.*

Philadelphia : J. B. Lippincott Company.

BATEMAN (MAY).

A VOLUME OF POEMS. With a title design by P. WILSON
STEER. [*Shortly.*

BINYON (LAURENCE).

LYRIC POEMS, with title page by SELWYN IMAGE. Sq.
16mo. 5s. *net.*

"This little volume of LYRIC POEMS displays a grace of fancy, a spontaneity
and individuality of inspiration, and a felicitous command of metre and diction, which
lift the writer above the average of the minor singers of our time. . . . We may
expect much from the writer of 'An April Day,' or of the strong concluding lines on
the present age from a piece entitled ' Present and Future.' "—*Times.*

" The product of a definite and sympathetic personality."—*Globe.*

" The impression that this volume makes upon us is that the writer has caught
the spirit of Matthew Arnold, and that in no common degree. . . . Quite
Titianesque in its force and colour."—*Spectator.*

BLACKMORE (R. D.)

FRINGILLA : OR, SOME TALES IN VERSE. By the Author
of "Lorna Doone." With Eleven full-page Illustrations
and numerous vignettes and initials by LOUIS FAIRFAX-
MUCKLEY and Three by JAMES W. R. LINTON.
Crown 8vo. 10s. *net.*

Also 30 copies L. P. (25 for sale) on hand-made foolscap
4to. £1. 1s. *net.*

*(Quorsum haec ? Non potui qualem Philomela querelam ; Sed
fringilla velut pipitabunda, vagor.)*

BLACKMORE (R. D.)—continued.

. . . "This volume of poems, with its fantastic title, is one of the literary events of the hour."—*Queen.*

"Mr. Blackmore, the novelist, has always been known among his friends as poet and scholar too. The first book he published, at the age of thirty-two, was a translation of the first two books of the 'Georgics.' That was seven years before he wrote 'Lorna Doone,' which made him famous. He is now about to appeal to the public as poet on his own account with a book of Tales in Verse, entitled 'Fringilla.' . . . Some day perhaps he will give us some Georgics of his own, informed and inspired by the experience, insight, and affections gained as a market-gardener now of considerable standing.' —*St. James's Gazette.*

BOURDILLON (F. W.).

A LOST GOD : a Poem in Three Books. With illustrations by H. J. FORD. Printed at the CHISWICK PRESS. 500 copies. 8vo. 6s. net. [*Very few remain.* Also 50 copies, royal 8vo., L. P. 17s. 6d. net.

" A graceful presentation in blank verse, with slight but effective dramatic setting, of the legend of the death of Pan on the morning that Christ began his teaching."—*Times.*

[Isham Facsimile Reprint.]

BRETON (NICHOLAS).

NO WHIPPINGE, NOR TRIPPINGE, BUT A KINDE FRIENDLY SNIPPINGE. London, 1601. A Facsimile Reprint, with the original Borders to every page, with a Bibliographical Note by CHARLES EDMONDS. 200 copies, printed on hand-made paper at the CHISWICK PRESS. 12mo. 3s. 6d. net. Also 50 copies Large Paper. 5s. net.

Facsimile reprint from the semi-unique copy discovered in the autumn of 1867 by Mr. Charles Edmonds in a disused lumber room at Lamport Hall, Northants (Sir Charles E. Isham's), and purchased lately by the British Museum authorities. When Dr. A. B. Grosart collected Breton's Works a few years ago for his " Chertsey Worthies Library," he was forced to confess that certain of Breton's most coveted books were missing and absolutely unavailable. The semi-unique example under notice was one of these.

C MAJOR OF LIFE (THE).

By a NEW WRITER. Post 8vo. 3s. 6d. net.

[*In preparation.*

CARMAN (BLISS) & RICHARD HOVEY.

SONGS FROM VAGABONDIA. With Decorations by TOM B. METEYARD. Fcap. 8vo. 5s. net.

Boston : Copeland & Day.

" The Authors of the small joint volume called 'Songs from Vagabondia,' have an unmistakable right to the name of poet. These little snatches have the spirit of a

CARMAN (BLISS) & RICHARD HOVEY—continued.

gipsy Omar Khayyám. They have always careless verve, and often careless felicity; they are masculine and rough, as roving songs should be. . . . Here, certainly, is the poet's soul. . . . You have the whole spirit of the book in such an unforgetable little lyric as 'In the House of Idiedaily.' . . We refer the reader to the delightful little volume itself, which comes as a welcome interlude amidst the highly wrought introspective poetry of the day."—FRANCIS THOMPSON, in *Merry England*.

"Bliss Carman is the author of a delightful volume of verse, 'Low Tide on Grand Pré,' and Richard Hovey is the foremost of the living poets of America, with the exception, perhaps, of Bret Harte and Joaquim Miller, whose names are more familiar. He sounds a deeper note than either of these, and deals with loftier themes."—*Dublin Express*.

"Both possess the power of investing actualities with fancy, and leaving them none the less actual; of setting the march music of the vagabond's feet to words; of being comrades with nature, yet without presumption. And they have that charm, rare in writers of verse, of drawing the reader into the fellowship of their own zest and contentment."—*Athenæum*.

CHAPMAN (ELIZABETH RACHEL).

A LITTLE CHILD'S WREATH: A Sonnet Sequence. With title page and cover designed by SELWYN IMAGE. Second Edition. Sq. 16mo., green buckram. 3s. 6d. net.
New York: Dodd, Mead & Company.

"Contains many tender and pathetic passages, and some really exquisite and subtle touches of childhood nature. . . . The average excellence of the sonnets is undoubted."—*Spectator*.

"In these forty pages of poetry . . . we have a contribution inspired by grief for the loss of a child of seven, which is not unworthy to take its place even beside 'In Memoriam.' . . . Miss Chapman has ventured upon sacred ground, but she has come off safely, with the inspiration of a divine sympathy in her soul, and with lips touched with the live coal from the altar on which glows the flame of immortal love."—W. T. STEAD, in *The Review of Reviews*.

"Full of a very solemn and beautiful but never exaggerated sentiment."—LOGROLLER, in *Star*.

"While they are brimming with tenderness and tears, they are marked with the skilled workmanship of the real poet."—*Glasgow Herald*.

"Evidently describes very real and intense sorrow. Its strains of tender sympathy will appeal specially to those whose hearts have been wrung by the loss of a young child, and the verses are touching in their simplicity."—*Morning Post*.

"Re-assures us on its first page by its sanity and its simple tenderness."—*Bookman*.

COLERIDGE (HON. STEPHEN).

THE SANCTITY OF CONFESSION: A Romance. 2nd edition. Printed by CLOWES & SON. 250 copies. Cr. 8vo. 3s. net.   [*Very few remain.*

"Mr. Stephen Coleridge's sixteenth-century romance is well and pleasantly written. The style is throughout in keeping with the story; and we should imagine that the historical probabilities are well observed."—*Pall Mall Gazette*.

Mr. GLADSTONE writes:—"I have read the singularly well told story. . . . It opens up questions both deep and dark; it cannot be right to accept in religion or anything else a secret which destroys the life of an innocent fellow creature."

CORBIN (JOHN).

THE ELIZABETHAN HAMLET: A Study of the Sources, and of Shakspere's Environment, to show that the Mad Scenes had a Comic Aspect now Ignored. With a Prefatory Note by F. YORK POWELL, Professor of Modern History at the University of Oxford. Small 4to. 3s. 6d. net.

New York: Charles Scribner's Sons.

This book is a study of the sources of "Hamlet," and of Shakespeare's environment, with the object of showing that the mad scenes in the play had a comic aspect now ignored. Mr. Corbin's general standpoint is that Shakespeare naturally wrote the drama for Elizabethan audiences. They in their time saw jest in what would seem to us only the severest tragedy. What he wishes to get at is the comedy in "Hamlet" according to the Elizabethan point of view.

. . . "When we add that so competent a judge as Professor York Powell expresses his belief in a Prefatory Note that Mr. Corbin has 'got hold of a truth that has not been clearly, if at all, expressed in our Elizabethan studies—to wit, that the 16th century audience's point of view, and, of necessity, the playwright's treatment of his subject, were very different from ours of to-day in many matters of mark'—and express our own concurrence in this, we have said enough to recommend Mr. Corbin's little book to the attention of all Shakespearian students."—*Times.*

CROSSING (WILLIAM).

THE ANCIENT CROSSES OF DARTMOOR; with a Description of their Surroundings. With 11 plates. 8vo. cloth. 4s. 6d. net. [*Very few remain.*

DAVIES (R. R.).

SOME ACCOUNT OF THE OLD CHURCH AT CHELSEA AND OF ITS MONUMENTS. [*In preparation.*

DE GRUCHY (AUGUSTA).

UNDER THE HAWTHORN, AND OTHER VERSES. With Frontispiece by WALTER CRANE. Printed at the RUGBY PRESS. 300 copies. Cr. 8vo. 5s. net. Also 30 copies on Japanese vellum. 15s. net.

"Melodious in metre, graceful in fancy, and not without spontaneity of inspiration."—*Times.*

"Very tender and melodious is much of Mrs. De Gruchy's verse. Rare imaginative power marks the dramatic monologue 'In the Prison Van.'"—*Speaker.*

"Distinguished by the attractive qualities of grace and refinement, and a purity of style that is as refreshing as a limpid stream in the heat of a summer's noon. . . . The charm of these poems lies in their naturalness, which is indeed an admirable quality in song."—*Saturday Review.*

DESTRÉE (OLIVIER GEORGES).

POÈMES SANS RIMES. Imprimé à Londres aux Presses de Chiswick, d'apres les dessins de HERBERT P. HORNE. 25 copies for sale. Square cr. 8vo. 8s. 6d. net.

DIVERSI COLORES SERIES.

See HORNE.

DOWSON (ERNEST).

DILEMMAS : Stories and Studies in Sentiment. (A Case of Conscience.—The Diary of a Successful Man.—An Orchestral Violin.—The Statute of Limitations.— Souvenirs of an Egoist). Crown 8vo. 3s. 6d. *net.*

POEMS (*Diversi Colores* Series). With a title design by H. P. HORNE. Printed at the CHISWICK PRESS, on hand-made paper. 16mo. 5s. *net.* [*Shortly.*

"Mr. Dowson's contributions to the two series of the *Rhymer's Book* were subtle and exquisite poems. He has a touch of Elizabethan distinction. . . . Mr. Dowson's stories are very remarkable in quality."—*Boston Literary World.*

FIELD (MICHAEL).

SIGHT AND SONG (Poems on Pictures). Printed by CONSTABLES. 400 copies. 12mo. 5s. *net.*
[*Very few remain.*

"This is a fascinating little volume ; one that will give to many readers a new interest in the examples of pictorial art with which it deals. Certainly, in the delight in the beauty of the human form, and of the fair shows of earth, and sea, and sky which it manifests, and in the harmonious verbal expression which this delight has found, the book is one of the most Keats-like things that has been produced since Keats himself took his seat among the immortals."—*Academy.*

"The verses have a sober grace and harmony, and the truth and poetic delicacy of the work is only realised on a close comparison with the picture itself. It is soothing and pleasant to participate in such leisurely degustation and enjoyment, such insistent penetration, for these poems are far removed from mere description, and the renderings, though somewhat lacking in the sense of humour, show both courage and poetical imagination."—*Westminster Review.*

STEPHANIA: A TRIALOGUE IN THREE ACTS. Frontis-piece, colophon, and ornament for binding designed by SELWYN IMAGE. Printed by FOLKARD & SON. 250 copies (200 for sale). Pott 4to. 6s. *net.*
[*Very few remain.*

"We have true drama in 'Stephania.' . . . . Stephania, Otho, and Sylvester II., the three persons of the play, are more than mere names. . . . Besides great effort, commendable effort, there is real greatness in this play ; and the blank verse is often sinewy and strong with thought and passion."—*Speaker.*

"'Stephania' is striking in design and powerful in execution. It is a highly dramatic 'trialogue' between the Emperor Otho III., his tutor Gerbert, and Stephania, the widow of the murdered Roman Consul, Crescentius. The poem contains much fine work, and is picturesque and of poetical accent. . . ."—*Westminster Review.*

A QUESTION OF MEMORY: A PLAY IN FOUR ACTS. 100 copies only. 8vo. 5s. *net.* [*Very few remain.*

GALTON (ARTHUR).

ESSAYS UPON MATTHEW ARNOLD (*Diversi Colores* Series). Printed at the CHISWICK PRESS on hand-made paper. Cr. 8vo.   5*s. net.*   [*In preparation.*

GASKIN (MRS. ARTHUR).

AN A.B.C. BOOK.   Rhymed and Pictured by MRS. ARTHUR GASKIN.   [*In preparation.*

HAKE (DR. T. GORDON, "The Parable Poet.")

MADELINE, AND OTHER POEMS.   Crown 8vo.   5*s. net.*

Transferred to the present Publisher.

"The ministry of the angel Daphne to her erring human sister is frequently related in strains of pure and elevated tenderness. Nor does the poet who can show so much delicacy fail in strength.   The description of Madeline as she passes in trance to her vengeance is full of vivid pictures and charged with tragic feeling.
The individuality of the writer lies in his deep sympathy with whatever affects the being and condition of man. . . .   Taken as a whole, the book has high and unusual claims."—*Athenæum.*

"I have been reading 'Madeline' again. For sheer originality, both of conception and of treatment, I consider that it stands alone."—MR. THEODORE WATTS.

PARABLES AND TALES.   (Mother and Child.—The Cripple.—The Blind Boy.—Old Morality.—Old Souls.—The Lily of the Valley.—The Deadly Nightshade.—The Poet).   With a Biographical Sketch by THEODORE WATTS.   9 illustrations by ARTHUR HUGHES.   New Edition.   Crown 8vo.   3*s. 6d. net.*

"The qualities of Dr. Gordon Hake's work were from the first fully admitted and warmly praised by one of the greatest of contemporary poets, who was also a critic of exceptional acuteness—Rossetti.   Indeed, the only two review articles which Rossetti ever wrote were written on two of Dr. Hake's books: 'Madeline,' which he reviewed in the *Academy* in 1871, and 'Parables and Tales,' which he reviewed in the *Fortnightly* in 1873. Many eminent critics have expressed a decided preference for 'Parables and Tales' to Dr. Hake's other works, and it had the advantage of being enriched with the admirable illustrations of Arthur Hughes."—*Saturday Review,* January, 1895.

"The piece called 'Old Souls' is probably secure of a distinct place in the literature of our day, and we believe the same may be predicted of other poems in the little collection just issued. . . .   Should Dr. Hake's more restricted, but lovely and sincere contributions to the poetry of real life not find the immediate response they deserve, he may at least remember that others also have failed to meet at once with full justice and recognition.   But we will hope for good encouragement to his present and future work; and can at least ensure the lover of poetry that in these simple pages he shall find not seldom a humanity limpid and pellucid—the well-spring of a true heart, with which his tears must mingle as with their own element.

"Dr. Hake has been fortunate in the beautiful drawings which Mr. Arthur Hughes has contributed to his little volume.   No poet could have a more congenial yoke-fellow than this gifted and imaginative artist."—D. G. ROSSETTI, in the *Fortnightly.* 1873.

HALLAM (ARTHUR).

THE POEMS OF ARTHUR HENRY HALLAM, together with his Essay "ON SOME OF THE CHARACTERISTICS OF MODERN POETRY, AND ON THE LYRICAL POEMS OF ALFRED TENNYSON," reprinted from the *Englishman's Magazine*, 1831, edited, with an introduction, by RICHARD LE GALLIENNE. 550 copies (500 for sale). Small 8vo. 5s. net.

New York: Macmillan & Co.

Many of these Poems are of great Tennysonian interest, having been addressed to Alfred, Charles, and Emily Tennyson.

HAMILTON (COL. IAN).

THE BALLAD OF HADJI, AND OTHER POEMS. With etched frontispiece by WILLIAM STRANG. Printed at the CHISWICK PRESS. 550 copies. 12mo. 3s. net.

Transferred by the Author to the present Publisher.

"Here is a dainty volume of clear, sparkling verse. The thought is sparkling, and the lines limpid and lightly flowing."—*Scotsman*.

HARPER (CHARLES G.)

REVOLTED WOMAN: PAST, PRESENT, AND TO COME. Printed by STRANGEWAYS. Illustrated with numerous original drawings and facsimiles by the Author. Crown 8vo. 5s. net.

"Mr. Harper, like a modern John Knox, denounces the monstrous regiment of women, making the ' New Woman' the text of a discourse that bristles with historical instances and present day portraits."—*Saturday Review*.

" The illustrations are distinctly clever."—*Publishers' Circular*.

HEMINGWAY (PERCY).

OUT OF EGYPT: Stories from the Threshold of the East. Cover design by GLEESON WHITE. Crown 8vo. 3s. 6d. net.

"This is a strong book."—*Academy*.

"This is a remarkable book. Egyptian life has seldom been portrayed from the inside. . . . The author's knowledge of Arabic, his sympathy with the religion of Islam, above all his entire freedom from Western prejudice, have enabled him to learn more of what modern Egypt really is than the average Englishman could possibly acquire in a lifetime at Cairo or Port Said."—*African Review*.

"A lively and picturesque style. . . . undoubted talent."—*Manchester Guardian*.

" But seldom that the first production o. an author is so mature and so finished in style as this. . . . The sketches are veritable spoils of the Egyptians—gems of sproe in a setting of clear air, sharp outlines, and wondrous skies.—*Morning Leader*.

HEMINGWAY (PERCY)—*continued.*

"This book places its author amongst those writers from whom lasting work of high aim is to be expected."—*The Star.*

"The tale . . . is treated with daring directness. . . An impressive and pathetic close to a story told throughout with arresting strength and simplicity."—*Daily News.*

"Genuine power and pathos."—*Pall Mall Gazette.*

THE HAPPY WANDERER (Poems). With title design by Charles I. ffoulkes. Printed at the CHISWICK PRESS, on hand-made paper. Sq. 16mo. 5s. *net.* [*In the press.*

HICKEY (EMILY H.).

A VOLUME OF POEMS. [*In preparation.*

VERSE TALES, LYRICS AND TRANSLATIONS. Printed at the ARNOLD PRESS. 300 copies. Imp. 16mo. 5s. *net.* [*Very few remain.*

'Miss Hickey's 'Verse Tales, Lyrics, and Translations' almost invariably reach a high level of finish and completeness. The book is a string of little rounded pearls.—*Athenæum.*

HINKSON (HENRY A.).

DUBLIN VERSES. By MEMBERS OF TRINITY COLLEGE. Selected and Edited by H. A. HINKSON, late Scholar of Trinity College, Dublin. Pott 4to. 5s. *net.* *Dublin: Hodges, Figgis & Co., Limited.*

Includes contributions by the following :—Aubrey de Vere, Sir Stephen de Vere, Oscar Wilde, J. K. Ingram, A. P. Graves, J. Todhunter, W. E. H. Lecky, T. W. Rolleston, Edward Dowden, G. A. Greene, Savage-Armstrong, Douglas Hyde, R. Y. Tyrrell, G. N. Plunkett, W. Macneile Dixon, William Wilkins, George Wilkins, and Edwin Hamilton.

"A pleasant volume of contemporary Irish Verse. . . A judicious selection."—*Times.*

"Wherever there is a group of Irish readers in near or far-off lands, these 'Dublin Verses' will be sure to command attention and applause."—*Glasgow Herald.*

HINKSON (KATHARINE).

SLOES ON THE BLACKTHORN : A VOLUME OF IRISH STORIES. Crown 8vo., 3s. 6d. *net.* [*In preparation.*

"HOBBY HORSE (THE)."

AN ILLUSTRATED ART MISCELLANY. Edited by HERBERT P. HORNE. The Fourth Number of the New Series will shortly appear, after which MR. MATHEWS will publish all the numbers in a volume, price £1. 1s. *net.* *Boston: Copeland & Day.*

HORNE (HERBERT P.)

DIVERSI COLORES: Poems. Vignette, &c., designed by the Author. Printed at the CHISWICK PRESS. 250 copies. 16mo. 5s. net.

Transferred by the Author to the present Publisher.

" In these few poems Mr. Horne has set before a tasteless age, and an extravagant age, examples of poetry which, without fear or hesitation, we consider to be of true and pure beauty."—*Anti-Jacobin.*

" With all his fondness for sixteenth century styles and themes, Mr. Horne is yet sufficiently individual in his thought and manner. Much of his sentiment is quite latter-day in tone and rendering; he is a child of his time."—*Globe.*

" Mr. Horne's work is almost always carefully felicitous and may be compared with beautiful filagree work in verse. He is fully, perhaps too fully, conscious of the value of restraint, and is certainly in need of no more culture in the handling of verse —of such verse as alone he cares to work in. He has already the merits of a finished artist—or, at all events, of an artist who is capable of the utmost finish."—*Pall Mall Gazette.*

The SERIES OF BOOKS begun in "DIVERSI COLORES" by Mr. HERBERT P. HORNE, will continue to be published by Mr. Elkin Mathews.

The intention of the series is to give, in a collected and sometimes revised form, Poems and Essays by various writers, whose names have hitherto been chiefly associated with the *Hobby Horse.* The series will be edited by Mr. HERBERT P. Horne, and will contain:

No. II. POEMS AND CAROLS. By SELWYN IMAGE.
[*Just published.*

No. III. ESSAYS UPON MATTHEW ARNOLD. By ARTHUR GALTON. [*Immediately.*

No. IV. POEMS. By ERNEST DOWSON.

No. V. THE LETTERS AND PAPERS OF ADAM LEGENDRE.

Each volume will contain a new title-page and ornaments designed by the Editor; and the volumes of verse will be uniform with "Diversi Colores."

HORTON (ALICE).

POEMS. [*Shortly.*

HUEFFER (OLIVER F. MADOX).

SONNETS AND POEMS. With a frontispiece. [*Shortly.*

HUGHES (ARTHUR).
   See HAKE.

HUNT (LEIGH).
   A VOLUME OF ESSAYS now collected for the first time.
   Edited with a critical Introduction by R. W. M.
   JOHNSON.   [In the press.

IMAGE (SELWYN).
   POEMS AND CAROLS. (Diversi Colores Series.—New
      Volume). Title design by H. P. HORNE. Printed
      on hand-made paper at the CHISWICK PRESS. 16mo.
      5s. net.   [Just ready.

   "Among the artists who have turned poets will shortly have to be reckoned Mr.
Selwyn Image. A volume of poems from his pen will be published by Mr. Elkin
Mathews before long. Those who are acquainted with Mr. Selwyn Image's work
will expect to find a real and deep poetic charm in this book."—Daily Chronicle.

   "No one else could have done it (i.e., written 'Poems and Carols') in just this
way, and the artist himself could have done it in no other way." "A remarkable
impress of personality, and this personality of singular rarity and interest. Every
piece is perfectly composed; the 'mental cartooning,' to use Rossetti's phrase, has
been adequately done . . . an air of grave and homely order . . . a union of
quaint and subtly simple homeliness, with a somewhat abstract severity. . . . It
is a new thing, the revelation of a new poet. . . . Here is a book which may be
trusted to outlive most contemporary literature."—Saturday Review.

   "An intensely personal expression of a personality of singular charm, gravity,
fancifulness, and interest; work which is alone among contemporary verse alike in
regard to substance and to form . . . comes with more true novelty than any
book of verse published in England for some years."—Athenæum.

   "Some men seem to avoid fame as sedulously as the majority seek it. Mr. Selwyn
Image is one of these. He has achieved a charming fame by his very shyness and
mystery. His very name has a look of having been designed by the Century Guild,
and it was certainly first published in The Century Guild Hobby Horse."—The Realm.

   "In the tiny little volume of verse, 'Poems and Carols,' by Selwyn Image,
we discern a note of spontaneous inspiration, a delicate and graceful fancy, and
considerable, but unequal, skill of versification. The Carols are skilful reproductions
of that rather archaic form of composition, devotional in tone and felicitous in
sentiment. Love and nature are the principal themes of the Poems. It is difficult
not to be hackneyed in the treatment of such themes, but Mr. Image successfully
overcomes the difficulty."—The Times.

   "The Catholic movement in literature, a strong reality to-day in England as in
France, if working within narrow limits, has its newest interpretation in Mr. Selwyn
Image's 'Poems and Carols.' Of course the book is charming to look at and to
handle, since it is his. The Chiswick Press and Mr. Mathews have helped him to
realize his design."—The Sketch.

ISHAM FACSIMILE REPRINTS; Nos. III. and IV.
   See BRETON and SOUTHWELL.

   *** New Elizabethan Literature at the British Museum, see
The Times, 31 August, 1894, also Notes and Queries, Sept., 1894.

[By the Author of *The Art of Thomas Hardy*].

JOHNSON (LIONEL).

POEMS. With a title design and colophon by H. P. HORNE. Printed at the CHISWICK PRESS, on hand-made paper. Sq. post 8vo. 5s. *net.*

Also, 25 special copies at 15s. *net.*

Boston: Copeland and Day.

" Full of delicate fancy, and display much lyrical grace and felicity."—*Times.*

"An air of solidity, combined with something also of severity, is the first impression one receives from these pages. . . . The poems are more massive than most lyrics are; they aim at dignity and attain it. This is, we believe, the first book of verse that Mr. Johnson has published; and we would say, on a first reading, that for a first book it was remarkably mature. And so it is, in its accomplishment, its reserve of strength, its unfaltering style. . . . Whatever form his writing takes, it will be the expression of a rich mind, and a rare talent."—*Saturday Review.*

"Mr. Lionel Johnson's poems have the advantage of a two-fold inspiration. Many of these austere strains could never have been written if he had not been steeped in the most golden poetry of the Greeks; while, on the other hand, side by side with the mellifluous chanting, there comes another note, mild, sweet. and unsophisticated—the very bird-note of Celtic poetry. And then again one comes on a very ripe and affluent, as of one who has spoiled the very goldenest harvests of song of cultivated ages. . . . Mr. Johnson's poetry is concerned with lofty things and is never less than passionately sincere. It is sane, high-minded, and full of felicities." —*Illustrated London News.*

"The most obvious characteristics of Mr. Johnson's verse are dignity and distinction; but beneath these one feels a passionate poetic impulse, and a grave fascinating music passes from end to end of the volume."—*Realm.*

"It is at once stately and passionate, austere, and free. His passion has a sane mood: his fire a white heat. . . . Once again it is the Celtic spirit that makes for higher things. Mr. Johnson's muse is concerned only with the highest. Her flight is as of a winged thing, that goes 'higher still and higher,' and has few flutterings near earth."—*Irish Daily Independent.*

JOHNSON (EFFIE).

IN THE FIRE, AND OTHER FANCIES. With frontispiece by WALTER CRANE. Imperial 16mo. 3s. 6d. *net.*

LAMB (CHARLES).

BEAUTY AND THE BEAST. With an Introduction by ANDREW LANG. Facsimile Reprint of the rare First Edition. *With 8 choice stipple engravings in brown ink, after the original plates.* Royal 16mo. 3s. 6d. *net.*

Transferred to the present Publisher.

MARSON (REV. C. L.).

A VOLUME OF SHORT STORIES.   [*In preparation.*

MARSTON (PHILIP BOURKE).

A LAST HARVEST: LYRICS AND SONNETS FROM THE BOOK OF LOVE. Edited, with Biographical Sketch, by LOUISE CHANDLER MOULTON. 500 copies. Printed by MILLER & SON. Post 8vo. 5s. net.

[*Very few remain.*

Also 50 copies on hand-made L.P. 10s. 6d. net.

[*Very few remain.*

"Among the sonnets with which the volume concludes, there are some fine examples of a form of verse in which all competent authorities allow that Marston excelled. 'The Breadth and Beauty of the Spacious Night,' 'To All in Haven,' 'Friendship and Love,' 'Love's Deserted Palace'—these, to mention no others, have the 'high seriousness' which Matthew Arnold made the test of true poetry."—*Athenæum.*

"Mrs. Chandler Moulton's biography is a beautiful piece of writing, and her estimate of his work—a high estimate—is also a just one."—*Black and White.*

MASON (A. E. W.).

A ROMANCE OF WASTDALE. Crown 8vo. 3s. 6d. net.

[*Immediately.*

MORRISON (G. E.).

ALONZO QUIXANO, otherwise DON QUIXOTE: being a dramatization of the Novel of CERVANTES, and especially of those parts which he left unwritten. Cr. 8vo. 1s. net.

MUSA CATHOLICA.

Selected and Edited by MRS. WILLIAM SHARP.

[*In preparation.*

MURRAY (ALMA).

PORTRAIT AS BEATRICE CENCI. With Critical Notice containing Four Letters from ROBERT BROWNING. 8vo. 2s. net.

NOEL (HON. RODEN).

MY SEA, and other posthumous Poems. With an Introduction by STANLEY ADDLESHAW. [*In preparation.*

SELECTED LYRICS FROM THE WORKS OF THE LATE HON. RODEN NOEL. With a Biographical and Critical Essay by PERCY ADDLESHAW. Illustrated with Two Portraits, including a reproduction of the famous picture by W. B. RICHMOND, A.R.A. [*In preparation.*

NOEL (HON. RODEN)—continued.

POOR PEOPLE'S CHRISTMAS. Printed at the AYLESBURY
PRESS. 250 copies. 16mo. 1s. net.
[Very few remain.

"Displays the author at his best. . . . . Mr. Noel always has something
to say worth saying, and his technique—though like Browning, he is too intent upon
idea to bestow all due care upon form—is generally sufficient and sometimes
masterly. We hear too seldom from a poet of such deep and kindly sympathy."—
Sunday Times.

O'SULLIVAN (VINCENT).

POEMS. With a title-design by SELWYN IMAGE.
[In preparation.

POWELL (F. YORK).

See CORBIN.

PROBYN (MAY).

PANSIES : A BOOK OF POEMS. With a title-page and cover
design by MINNIE MATHEWS. Fcap. 8vo. 3s. 6d. net.

> "De mon jardin, voyageur,
> Vous me demandez une fleur?
> Cueillez toujours—mais je n'ai,
> Voyageur, que des pensées."

"Miss Probyn's new volume is a slim one, but rare in quality. She is no mere
pretty verse maker ; her spontaneity and originality are beyond question, and so far
as colour and picturesqueness go, only Mr. Francis Thompson rivals her among the
English Catholic poets of to-day."—*Sketch.*

"This too small book is a mine of the purest poetry, very holy, and very
refined, and removed as far as possible from the tawdry or the common-place."—*Irish
Monthly.*

"The religious poems are in their way perfect, with a tinge of the mysticism
one looks for in the poetry of two centuries ago, but so seldom meets with nowadays."
—*Catholic Times.*

"Full of a delicate devotional sentiment and much metrical felicity."—*Times.*

RHYMERS' CLUB, THE SECOND BOOK OF THE.

Contributions by E. DOWSON, E. J. ELLIS, G. A. GREENE,
A. HILLIER, LIONEL JOHNSON, RICHARD LE GAL-
LIENNE, VICTOR PLARR, E. RADFORD, E. RHYS,
T. W. ROLLESTONE, ARTHUR SYMONS, J. TOD-
HUNTER, W. B. YEATS. Printed by MILLER & SON.
500 copies (of which 400 are for sale). 16mo. 5s. net.
50 copies on hand-made L.P. 10s. 6d. net.

New York: Dodd, Mead & Co.

"The work of twelve very competent verse writers, many of them not unknown
to fame. This form of publication is not a new departure exactly, but it is a recurrence to the excellent fashion of the Elizabethan age, when 'England's Helicon, '

RHYMERS' CLUB, SECOND BOOK OF THE—continued.

Davison's ' Poetical Rhapsody,' and 'Phœnix Nest,' with scores of other collections, contained the best songs of the best song-writers of that tuneful epoch."—*Black and White.*

"The future of these thirteen writers, who have thus banded themselves together, will be watched with interest. Already there is fulfilment in their work, and there is much promise."—*Speaker.*

"In the intervals of Welsh rarebit and stout provided for them at the ' Cheshire Cheese,' in Fleet Street, the members of the Rhymers' Club have produced some very pretty poems, which Mr. Elkin Mathews has issued in his notoriously dainty manner."—*Pall Mall Gazette.*

ROBERTSON-HICKS (MAUDE).
SPRING VOICES.   [*Shortly.*

ROTHENSTEIN (WILL).
OCCASIONAL PORTRAITS.   With comments on the Personages by various writers.   [*In preparation.*

SCHAFF (DR. P.).
LITERATURE AND POETRY: Papers on Dante, Latin Hymns, &c.   Portrait and Plates.   100 copies only. 8vo.   10s. *net.*   [*Very few remain.*

SCULL (W. D.).
THE GARDEN OF THE MATCHBOXES, and other Stories. Crown 8vo.   3s. 6d. *net.*   [*In preparation.*

STRANGE (E. F.)
A BOOK OF THOUGHTS.   [*In preparation.*

[Isham Facsimile Reprint].

S[OUTHWELL] (R[OBERT]).
A FOVREFOVLD MEDITATION, OF THE FOURE LAST THINGS. COMPOSED IN A DIUINE POEME. By R. S. The author of S. Peter's complaint. London, 1606. A Facsimile Reprint, with a Bibliographical Note by CHARLES EDMONDS. 150 copies. Printed on hand-made paper at the CHISWICK PRESS. Roy. 16mo. 5s. *net.*
Also 50 copies, large paper. 7s. 6d. *net.*

Facsimile reprint from the unique fragment discovered in the autumn of 1867 by Mr. Charles Edmonds in a disused lumber room at Lamport Hall, Northants, and lately purchased by the British Museum authorities. This fragment supplies the first sheet of a previously unknown poem by Robert Southwell, the Roman Catholic poet, whose religious fervour lends a pathetic beauty to everything that he wrote, and future editors of Southwell's works will find it necessary to give it close study. The whole of the Poem has been completed from two MS. copies, which differ in the number of Stanzas.

SYMONDS (JOHN ADDINGTON).

IN THE KEY OF BLUE, AND OTHER PROSE ESSAYS. With cover designed by C. S. RICKETTS. Printed at the BALLANTYNE PRESS. Second Edition. Thick cr. 8vo. 8s. 6d. net.

New York : Macmillan & Co.

"The variety of Mr. Symonds' interests! Here are criticisms upon the Venetian Tiepolo, upon M. Zola, upon Mediæval Norman Songs, upon Elizabethan lyrics, upon Plato's and Dante's ideals of love; and not a sign anywhere, except may be in the last, that he has more concern for, or knowledge of, one theme than another. Add to these artistic themes the delighted records of English or Italian scenes, with their rich beauties of nature or of art, and the human passions that inform them. How joyous a sense of great possessions won at no man's hurt or loss must such a man retain."—*Daily Chronicle.*

"Some of the essays are very charming, in Mr. Symonds' best style, but the first one, that which gives its name to the volume, is at least the most curious of the lot."—*Speaker.*

"The other essays are the work of a sound and sensible critic."—*National Observer.*

"The literary essays are more restrained, and the prepared student will find them full of illumination and charm, while the descriptive papers have the attractiveness which Mr. Symonds always gives to work in this *genre.*"—MR. JAS. ASHCROFT NOBLE, in *The Literary World.*

TENNYSON (LORD).

See HALLAM,—VAN DYKE.

TODHUNTER (DR. JOHN).

A SICILIAN IDYLL. With a Frontispiece by WALTER CRANE. Printed at the CHISWICK PRESS. 250 copies. Imp. 16mo. 5s. net. 50 copies hand-made L.P. Fcap. 4to. 10s. 6d. net. [*Very few remain.*

"He combines his notes skilfully, and puts his own voice, so to speak, into them, and the music that results is sweet and of a pastoral tunefulness."—*Speaker.*

"The blank verse is the true verse of pastoral, quiet and scholarly, with frequent touches of beauty. The echoes of Theocritus and of the classics at large are modest and felicitous."—*Anti-Jacobin.*

"A charming little pastoral play in one act. The verse is singularly graceful, and many bright gems of wit sparkle in the dialogues."—*Literary World.*

"Well worthy of admiration for its grace and delicate finish, its clearness, and its compactness."—*Athenæum.*

Also the following works by the same Author transferred to the present Publisher, viz. :—LAURELLA, and other Poems, 5s. net.—ALCESTIS, a Dramatic Poem, 4s. net. —A STUDY OF SHELLEY, 5s. 6d. net.—FOREST SONGS, and other Poems, 3s. net.—THE BANSHEE, 3s. net.— HELENA IN TROAS, 2s. 6d. net.

TYNAN (KATHARINE).

See HINKSON.

VAN DYKE (HENRY).

THE POETRY OF TENNYSON.   Third Edition, enlarged. Cr. 8vo.   5s. 6d. net.

The additions consist of a Portrait, Two Chapters, and the Bibliography expanded.   The Laureate himself gave valuable aid in correcting various details.

"Mr. Elkin Mathews publishes a new edition, revised and enlarged, of that excellent work, 'The Poetry of Tennyson,' by Henry Van Dyke. The additions are considerable. It is extremely interesting to go over the bibliographical notes to see the contemptuous or, at best, contemptuously patronising tone of the reviewers in the early thirties gradually turning to civility, to a loud chorus of applause."—*Anti-Jacobin.*

"Considered as an aid to the study of the Laureate, this labour of love merits warm commendation. Its grouping of the poems, its bibliography and chronology, its catalogue of Biblical allusion and quotations, are each and all substantial accessories to the knowledge of the author."—DR. RICHARD GARNETT, in the *Illustrated London News.*

WATSON (E. H. LACON).

THE UNCONSCIOUS HUMOURIST, AND OTHER ESSAYS.

[*In preparation.*

[*Mr. Wedmore's Short Stories.   New and Uniform Issue. Crown 8vo., each Volume 3s. 6d. net.*]

WEDMORE (FREDERICK).

PASTORALS OF FRANCE.   Fourth Edition.   Crown 8vo. 3s. 6d. net.   [*Ready.*

New York: Charles Scribner's Sons.

"A writer in whom delicacy of literary touch is united with an almost disembodied fineness of sentiment."—*Athenaeum.*

"Of singular quaintness and beauty."—*Contemporary Review.*

"The stories are exquisitely told."—*The World.*

"Delicious idylls, written with Mr. Wedmore's fascinating command of sympathetic incident, and with his characteristic charm of style."—*Illustrated London News.*

"The publication of the 'Pastorals' may be said to have revealed, not only a new talent, but a new literary *genre.* . . The charm of the writing never fails."—*Bookman.*

"In their simplicity, their tenderness, their quietude, their truthfulness to the remote life that they depict, 'Pastorals of France' are almost perfect."—*Spectator.*

WEDMORE (FREDERICK)—continued.

RENUNCIATIONS. Third Edition. With a Portrait by J. J. SHANNON. Cr. 8vo. 3s. 6d. net. [*Ready.*

New York: Charles Scribner's Sons.

"These are clever studies in polite realism."—*Athenæum.*

"They are quite unusual. The picture of Richard Pelse, with his one moment of romance, is exquisite."—*St. James's Gazette.*

"'The Chemist in the Suburbs,' in 'Renunciations,' is a pure joy. . . . The story of Richard Pelse's life is told with a power not unworthy of the now disabled hand that drew for us the lonely old age of M. Parent."—MR. TRAILL, in *The New Review.*

"The book belongs to the highest order of imaginative work. 'Renunciations' are studies from the life—pictures which make plain to us some of the innermost workings of the heart."—*Academy.*

"Mr. Wedmore has gained for himself an enviable reputation. His style has distinction, has form. He has the poet's secret how to bring out the beauty of common things. . . 'The Chemist in the Suburbs,' in 'Renunciations,' is his masterpiece."—*Saturday Review.*

"We congratulate Mr. Wedmore on his vivid, wholesome, and artistic work, so full of suppressed feeling and of quiet strength."—*Standard.*

ENGLISH EPISODES. Second Edition. Cr. 8vo. 3s. 6d. net. [*Ready.*

New York: Charles Scribner's Sons.

"Distinction is the characteristic of Mr. Wedmore's manner. These things remain on the mind as things seen ; not read of."—*Daily News.*

"A penetrating insight, a fine pathos. Mr. Wedmore is a peculiarly fine and sane and carefully deliberate artist."—*Westminster Gazette.*

"In 'English Episodes' we have another proof of Mr. Wedmore's unique position among the writers of fiction of the day. We hardly think of his short volumes as ' stories,' but rather as life-secrets and hearts' blood, crystalised somehow, and, in their jewel-form, cut with exceeding skill by the hand of a master-workman.' . . The faultless episode of the 'Vicar of Pimlico' is the best in loftiness of purpose and keeness of interest ; but the ' Fitting Obsequies ' is its equal on different lines, and deserves to be a classic."—*World.*

"' English Episodes' are worthy successors of 'Pastorals' and 'Renunciations,' and with them should represent a permanent addition to Literature."—*Academy.*

There may also be had the Collected Edition (1893) of " Pastorals of France" and " Renunciations," with Title-page by John Fulleylove, R.I. 5s. net.

WICKSTEED (P. H., Warden of University Hall).

DANTE : SIX SERMONS.

*** A FOURTH EDITION. (Unaltered Reprint). Cr. 8vo. 2s. net.

"It is impossible not to be struck with the reality and earnestness with which Mr. Wicksteed seeks to do justice to what are the supreme elements of the *Commedia*, its spiritual significance, and the depth and insight of its moral teaching."—*Guardian.*

WYNNE (FRANCES).

WHISPER! A Volume of Verse. Fcap. 8vo. buckram. 2s. 6d. net.

Transferred by the Author to the present Publisher.

"A little volume of singularly sweet and graceful poems, hardly one of which can be read by any lover of poetry without definite pleasure, and everyone who reads either of them without is, we venture to say, unable to appreciate that play of light and shadow on the heart of man which is of the very essence of poetry."—*Spectator.*

"The book includes, to my humble taste, many very charming pieces, musical, simple, straightforward and *not* 'as sad as night.' It is long since I have read a more agreeable volume of verse, successful up to the measure of its aims and ambitions."—MR. ANDREW LANG, in *Longman's Magazine.*

YEATS (W. B.).

THE SHADOWY WATERS. A Poetic Play. [*In preparation.*

THE WIND AMONG THE REEDS (Poems). [*In preparation.*

MR. ELKIN MATHEWS *holds likewise the only copies of the following Books printed at the Private Press of the* REV. C. HENRY DANIEL, *Fellow of Worcester College, Oxford.*

BRIDGES (ROBERT).

THE GROWTH OF LOVE. Printed in Fell's old English type, on Whatman paper. 100 copies. Fcap. 4to. £2. 12s. 6d. net.

SHORTER POEMS. Printed in Fell's old English type, on Whatman paper. 100 copies. Five Parts. Fcap. 4to. £2. 12s. 6d. net.   [*Very few remain.*

HYMNI ECCLESIÆ CVRA HENRICI DANIEL.

Small 8vo. (1882), £1. 15s. net.

BLAKE HIS SONGS OF INNOCENCE

Sq. 16mo. 100 copies only. 12s. 6d. net.

MILTON ODE ON THE NATIVITY.

Sq. 16mo. 10s. 6d. net.

LONDON   VIGO STREET, W.